I0564632

Bearing Northeast

Bearing Northeast

by Henry Melton

Wire Rim Books
Hutto, Texas

WRB

This is a work of fiction. Names, events and locations, if they exist elsewhere, are used here fictitiously and any resemblance to real persons, places or events is entirely coincidental.

Bearing Northeast © 2011 by Henry Melton
All Rights Reserved

Printing History
First Edition: April 2011
ISBN 978-0-9802253-9-6

Website of Henry Melton
www.HenryMelton.com

Cover art by Fred Perry and Wes Hartman
Twitter avatars by Autumn-Angel

Printed in the United States of America

Wire Rim Books
www.wirerimbooks.com

For my Big Sister, Mary Solomon, who has always been there with encouragement through all my struggles.

Many people have helped make this work of fiction richer and deserve appreciation for their efforts.

The people who look over my shoulder and point out my mistakes:
Alan McConnell, Bettye Baldwin, Debra Andrews, Jim Dunn, Jonathan Andrews, Kim Uribes, Linda Elliott, Mary Ann Melton, Mary Solomon, Nick Wall, and Tom Stock

Other helpers and local experts:
Fran Gatti, Principal Ed Arnott, Sarah Power, Ashley Rae Dicks, and Loretta Bryant

Photo Credits:
Chapter 10 - Ryne Snow
Chapters 17, 21 - Sarah Power
Chapter 14 - Jeff Keyzer
Chapter 18 - NASA
Chapter 20
Brian Weedon, created with the STK software package from ATI

Contents

Biz and Seth's Rules

Rule One	We're still brother and sister, no matter what.
Rule Two	Until Seth is 18, Biz has parental authority.
Rule Three	No arguing in public. Don't give anyone ammunition to break us up.
Rule Four	I'll take care of you and you'll take care of me.
Rule Five	Whenever Biz takes a stand, she must explain.
Rule Six	Biz chooses her own boyfriends. Seth chooses his own girlfriends. No sniping.

Chapter 1: Bump in the Night

I'll miss the chill. Surf rumbled against the cliffs in the distance and Seth Palmer zipped up his jacket. He hadn't expected that. Two days ago, far to the south, high school had let out for the season. It had been sweltering at home in Fresno. But no time for second thoughts if he were going to get any chance to drive around. He stepped carefully in the dark, trying to avoid the creak of the wooden porch floorboards. Anything could wake his sister. Dim glow from the street light guided his sandals on the steps.

Pebble Beach Drive wasn't far, and it'd likely be the last time he'd be able to watch the moonlight on the offshore islands. Tomorrow would be pack-up-and-move. *I thought I hated this place. I guess I was wrong. You never realize what you have, until it's time to sell it.*

The trick would be to get the pickup out of the driveway without waking up his sister. Biz had promised that he'd be able to drive a little on this trip, but here they were, all 550 miles to Crescent City, and he hadn't put in any time at the wheel. He had a perfectly good provisional license, and she wouldn't let him use it. She said she trusted his driving, but she didn't act like it.

Crack! The muffled silence of the night was overturned. Almost like a close lightning strike, but with no flash, no boom, the crash came from behind the house. Seth pulled out his phone and used it to light his steps as he circled around to the back yard. A window lit up in the house. *Biz is awake.* He sighed. So much for sneaking out for a drive.

The big tree behind the retaining wall looked wrong. *A branch, a blow-down.* Maybe. The wind wasn't that strong, but maybe it had been cracked before. In the feeble glow of the phone's screen, he could see the fresh white scar where the limb had broken free.

"Seth! Are you out there?"

He sighed. "Yeah! The wind blew a big limb down. Something more to fix."

"Which tree?" Biz was silhouetted in the back porch doorway. She wrapped her robe tighter against the chill.

"The big one."

She shook her head. "Then it's not really on our property. I'll tell Fran, but we won't have to do anything about it.

"Now, Little Brother, you get back in here. It's going to be a big day tomorrow and I don't want you sleeping while leaving me to load the trailer. I let you sleep most of the drive here."

"I offered to drive!"

"That's not the point."

Partners, that's what we'd promised each other, but big sister is so very comfortable giving the orders.

"In a minute. I want to tell the gang."

She rolled her eyes and went back inside.

He switched to the Twitter app on his phone and entered:

	A big tree limb crashed behind the house. Wind didn't seem that strong.
SethPartner	

Moose was up.

	How big? Onea them sequoias?
moosenine	

SethPartner	@moosenine no one of the regular kind, oak or elm or something. Big branch tho
ClaraN1	@SethPartner We're invading the Iron Tower. Join in?
SethPartner	@ClaraN1 stuck on cell phone. In the dungeon unless I can swipe sis's laptop.
moosenine	@SethPartner when will you be back?
SethPartner	@moosenine maybe 4 days. Unload the house and haul it all south.
moosenine	@SethPartner hurry it up. Clara is too easy to beat.

ClaraN1	@moosenine I heard that! *stab from behind*
SethPartner	Gotta go. Getting cold.
moosenine	cold?

...

Biz was up at dawn, wrapping glasses in paper and packing them in a box. Seth made the rounds, stripping all the bedding and folding it into piles. He didn't have much enthusiasm for the job. Selling the summer house wasn't something that felt right. They needed the money, but it felt like a betrayal. Mom loved this place.

It's always the money. But he didn't want to think about that.

"I'm going to check the tree." She didn't hear him, but he didn't care. Morning was bright and not too cold. He headed straight for the fallen branch. By daylight, he could see that it wasn't wind damage.

But what caused this? There were two scars; the split where the branch broke from the trunk, but also another place where bark had been knocked free down to the white wood. *Something hit this.*

But that was crazy. The tree was well back from any roadway. The wind hadn't been strong enough to throw anything at the tree. The sky had been clear, no weather, just a solid sea breeze. What did that leave, a meteor? Something dropped from a plane?

That was a thought. The Jack McNamara city airport was just a quick walk down the road, but there hadn't been a plane in sight. He would have noticed.

But if something fell, it should still be here, shouldn't it?

He pushed his way into the tangle of branches, looking at the ground. *If it came down straight, it would have landed...here.*

And there was a fresh hole in the mulch. Dark soil made a circular pit several inches around, like the burrow of an earthworm, if they made earthworms the size of pythons. Hesitantly, he stuck his hand down in, until he was wrist deep in thick moist soil. He pulled it out and brushed off the clinging dirt. *Something has to be down there.*

He broke off a long stick and pushed it down, probing the depth. Two feet in, he hit something solid.

Maybe it was a meteor! Something could have come in, killed a lot of momentum breaking off the branch and then buried itself in the muddy soil.

He started scraping away at the hole with his hands. *I've got to dig it out. This could be something important, maybe even valuable.*

The idea of doing something, anything, important this summer started his heart pumping. He wasn't looking forward to a long hot dead summer in Fresno. All his plans had already collapsed, but this was new.

What if it was an asteroid chunk that I could sell to some university? Maybe we wouldn't have to get rid of the house? What if...?

He shook his head at the crazy thoughts. Even if it were valuable, Biz was right that it wasn't on their property. And even if there were someone to buy it, Fran the realtor was talking about closing the sale in just days. And they did need the money. They were on their own. *Just Biz and me.* If they couldn't free up the $45,000 equity locked up in this place they never used anymore, then they could lose their real home in Fresno. They decided to make the sale. It was reasonable. They'd get rid of one mortgage payment and have cash left in the bank. By the time he graduated, Biz claimed that she'd have a start on his college fund.

Seth shook off that thought as well. It was bad enough that after all that legal juggling his sister was his 'parent', but he didn't expect her to put him through college—not when she had to quit prior to finishing her own degree just to take care of him. He could live with being partners together, but he wasn't her baby. Rule One.

Then, his fingers touched metal, and all other thoughts vanished. He looked down into the darkness, but it was too deep and too narrow a hole to see anything. Working with his hands, his shoulder was nearly at ground level when he got a grip around the end. Metal, something manufactured–it had to be. It was too smooth to be anything else. How big was it? Would he need a shovel to widen the hole?

Ten more minutes work, and it shifted when he pushed it side to side. Soon, it started to come free. Luckily the mud wasn't muck, just damp, or suction would have held it even tighter.

It was filthy when it came out, smeared with mud streaks just like his arms, but it was obviously a metal canister of some kind. Six inches or so in diameter, it was about a foot and a half long, and the end that had hit the ground first was smashed and dented.

What is it? Where did it come from, and how did it get here?

	Guys, you're never going to believe what I just found.
SethPartner	

There was no immediate response. Which was just as well, because there would be questions and he didn't have any answers. He rubbed the mud smears off his phone's screen and stuck it back in his pocket.

He held the prize in both hands and tried to guess what it was. It wasn't too heavy. It felt like a capped off section of pipe rather than a solid metal slug.

Could it be a bomb? A high altitude plane might have dropped it, not just one coming into the local airport. There were no fins, and no obvious detonation plug on the end like he'd seen in old military shells. And if it were a bomb, then this one was a dud, because it certainly hit hard enough to set off an explosive.

Although, as bad as the deep end was mangled, he couldn't be sure what had been there before it hit the tree. It was just crumpled metal cauliflower under the mud.

He rubbed at the streaks. *Oh, ho! Numbers.* Embossed in the metal on the side was some kind of code; CA-445938.

He reached for his phone, then hesitated. He needed to clean his hands before he did anything else.

Biz caught him on the back porch, digging out the garden hose. "Don't pack that up yet. I'll want to wash out some things before we finish."

He nodded, "I'm just washing my hands."

Elizabeth Palmer had the kind of eyes grade school teachers use when students misbehave. "And you need it. What were you doing, making mud pies?"

She didn't even look at the cylinder on the ground at his feet.

"Ah, no, just looking at the tree limb that fell down."

"Well, clean up, dry off and come back in. We have to take the beds apart."

"Soon."

"I mean it."

"I can't come in like this!"

She went back inside. He washed the mud free and dried his hands on his jeans.

There was a reply on his phone.

nickyWhy	@SethPartner what are you doing up this early? My phone woke me upbwith your tweet.
SethPartner	@nickyWhy Hey, Nick. Do me a favor and google me up a steel cylinder 18 inches long, six inches diameter, serial number CA-445938.

 nickyWhy	@SethPartner okay, but give me time to eat breakfast and get to the computer. Can't think yet.
 SethPartner	@nickyWhy thx

Once Seth had the mud rinsed off of himself and the cylinder, he noticed that there was a fine line about an inch down from the undamaged end. Maybe it was an cap. It had a slightly different color than the rest of the cylinder. He struggled to twist it, but there was no give.

I need tools. He set it down on the porch and went inside. Biz was humming away as she unloaded the shelves and stuffed decorative, useless things into boxes. It had been awhile since he'd heard her hum or sing, or anything like that.

"Hey, what's that?"

She paused, and stared at the painted, wooden thing. "It's a Santa. See?" She turned it to face him. "I made it a long time ago. Mom kept it here."

He nodded, not knowing what to say. It was pretty ugly. She must have been in kindergarten when she made it.

"Have you broken down the beds yet?"

"Uh, no."

"Well, what have you been doing?"

"Working in the yard. Do you know where the tools are?"

"In the cabinets over the washing machine. You'd better unload the whole cabinet while you're at it."

He turned without a word. He couldn't think about the packing just yet. But the tools were where she said they were. None of the wrenches were large enough to fit the cylinder, so he took a putty knife and a hammer.

Three minutes later, Biz came out onto the porch.

"What in the world is that thing?"

Seth had it between his knees, trying to widen the gap by driving the knife in with the hammer.

"Uh. I found it. It's what broke the tree limb last night."

"Put that down. You don't know what's in it."

"Yes," he replied calmly, "hence the reason for opening it up."

"But it might be a bomb or something."

"A pretty poor one if it didn't go off after last night's impact. Look at this thing." He handed it to her.

She took it gingerly, then turned it over and looked at the mangled end. "This part isn't metal."

"I don't think the end cap is either. See the scratches I made. It's some kind of hard plastic. The middle part is steel, I think."

"You don't think it's a pipe bomb or something?"

"Have you ever seen a pipe bomb? You wouldn't make it with plastic. The pressure inside wouldn't ever get high enough for a worthwhile boom."

She grunted. He was the family expert with rockets and fireworks and other things that burned and blew up and she knew it. But, he could tell the puzzle was getting to her as well.

"Is it a screw-on cap?"

"Maybe, but I can't get a grip on it."

She looked down at the steps. "Let me try something."

Wedging the cap between the step and the riser of the next one, she held it down by putting her weight on it, while he gripped the main body with both hands and twisted. Slowly, it started to move.

"It's working!"

She stepped off of it and he twisted the cap the rest of the way off.

Inside, a digital display showed numbers. Biz shrieked and backed off.

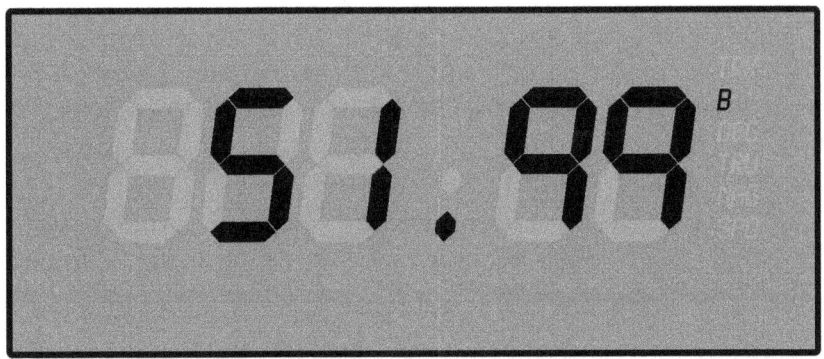

Chapter 2: Broken

It was a pale liquid crystal display, black digits on a gray background, just like an old digital clock.

51.99

"It's not a timer." He said it, and she nodded, but she was still flustered. For one thing, it wasn't counting down. For another the digits were wrong. Still, all the old movie scenes with a bomb with its counter working down to zero had come back in a split-second flash. He had jerked when he'd seen it too, although he wouldn't admit it.

"But what is it?"

She shook her head. "Give it to me."

Walking over to the sunlight, she set it down on a lawn table that was showing signs of rust. With expert hands she poked at the circuit that was barely exposed.

"Get my tool kit out of the glove compartment."

Seth dashed over to their silver gray pickup and found the little black leather case. With miniature screwdrivers and pliers, she opened it up. There was a circuit board, and a battery pack with four AA batteries, and hand-soldered to it was a little daughter circuit board that was broken.

Biz poked at the wires gently. She was the one who worked with electronics. "This used to be a GPS system, but it's been hacked somehow."

"What do you mean, hacked? Like new software?"

"Maybe. But it's hardware hacking. See this chip here?"

"The broken one?" It had a fracture down the length of it.

"Yes, that's a field programmable gate array. Someone reprogrammed the workings of this old GPS unit. Nice work, but since it's broken, I'll never be able to determine what's been done. It's stuck in some mode, but I can't tell what."

"Are you sure it's a GPS? There's no map."

"I said it's old. No map, but you can see the labels." She twisted it slightly in the light and he could see the inactive parts of the display, "'Degrees', 'True', 'Speed' and others. The 'B' is active, so I'd bet the number we see is a bearing."

He knew the term from his model rocket events out in the desert. A bearing was a compass direction to a destination.

"A bearing to what?"

"I dunno. It's target, or where it came from. Something."

Seth looked at the cylinder again with new eyes. "No motor. No fins. You can't tell me this thing could be steered. But why else would it have a GPS?"

"No, probably not. But there are more reasons for GPS than to control navigation. It could have been recording where it's been, like a weather balloon package."

"Could you read that data out? Find out where it came from?"

"Not without knowing a lot more about what the original GPS package was and its control codes. Anything I could do would likely wipe it out." She began re-securing the screws that held everything in place.

"But in any case, we need to get back to work packing up. Fran called and she's got a buyer who's interested and she needs us to get our stuff out so she can show it."

Seth took the cylinder and lightly replaced the cap. "Well, somebody owes us for a broken tree."

"Like I said, not our tree. Put that away and get to work on the beds."

...

| | Seth, I can't find any hits on your cylinder. #Googlefail |
| nickyWhy | |

moosenine	@SethPartner what did you find?
Seth Partner	@moosenine metal cylinder fell out of the sky and broke my tree. It's got some freaky electronics in it. Marked with CA-445938
moosenine	@SethPartner _Where_ are you again
SethPartner	Crescent City, California. Up at the top.
nickyWhy	Are there any airforce bases near you? Seems small for a bomb, tho
SethPartner	@nickyWhy Biz took it apart, found a GPS, but prob not a bomb. Thinks it might be weather balloon package.

moosenine	@SethPartner cool. Can you bring back with you?
SethPartner	@moosenine Unless I can sell it, sure.

Biz was waiting, so he couldn't spend time chatting. He took a moment to check his email, but there was nothing from Donna. It was like she'd vanished the day school closed. It looked like Nick had been right when he said to cut his losses and forget about her.

...

"I'm glad we got the unlimited data package on your phone. It's bad enough you spend all your time on it. I'd hate to have a huge spike in the bill just because we're out of town."

They were re-folding the bedding he'd done earlier because she said it wouldn't fit in the truck otherwise. He suspected it wouldn't matter, properly folded sheets were just a girl thing, but it wasn't something to argue over.

"The way I look at it, my cell usage is just a part of Rule Six. You shouldn't gripe."

Back during the dark days when Mom had just died and they decided to make do without any other adult trying to come in be a foster parent, they had established some ground rules for their new relationship. They were brother and sister, but she was also his guardian. The rules had changed and they knew it.

Rule Six said that she was free to choose her own boyfriends and he was free to choose his own girlfriends and there would be no sniping about their choices.

"I think that's a stretch. Do you even talk to Donna anymore?"

"No, and that is definitely a Rule Six violation."

"Sorry."

It looked like Donna Kelsey had made other arrangements for the summer. She was off to band camp with her circle of music friends and for the last month, it had been plain that she was spending more of her time with Druid, the trumpet player.

All because I don't have wheels. The image that remained in his head was Donna and a couple of her buddies laughing and climbing into Druid's old Buick Le Sabre and driving off after band practice. If she knew he had been there waiting for her, she didn't show it. The days were over when they killed time after school at Supreme Donuts or walked over the couple of blocks to the City College campus while waiting for Biz to get off work and come pick him up. Maybe Donna was a lost cause, now that she was more interested in touring the shopping centers or gushing over her visit to Druid's folk's country club, but it was clear her world had expanded past their old walking range. There was nothing he could do about that yet, but he didn't intend to be left out of the bigger world forever.

Donna wasn't his girl friend anymore. He was okay with it and as soon as Biz quit harping on that, the happier he'd be. Besides, he didn't really have anything in common with her anymore. He almost said so out loud, but that would have just given Biz more to gripe about.

He began bundling up more of the tools and loose items in the house. Better to work than feel sorry for himself. This summer was turning out to be a mess. Nothing he'd planned was happening. This trip to Crescent City had come up out of the blue. Biz had organized it, but she'd forgotten to fill him in on the details. Like the fact that her vacation slot, which couldn't be changed, trumped the paintball battle he'd been looking forward to for a month now.

"Biz, there's no room for anything more on the porch. Should we start loading up the pickup now?"

She put down the broom and looked over the collection. "There's a lot more stuff than I'd thought. We'll never get it to fit in the truck."

"Especially with the camper top. We shouldn't have brought that thing."

"Even without it, I don't think it'll all fit. We can't stack the truck bed twelve feet high and drive all the way back to Fresno that way."

"Some of it can just be thrown away."

There was no response. Biz had been saving every little thing, as if it were all made of gold. It was memories of Mom, he was sure of it. Maybe someday, he'd push the idea of getting rid of the pictures made of macaroni and glitter than had been gathering dust for ages, but he didn't feel like today was the day. They were getting rid of the summer house. That was a big enough step as it was.

She nodded at his phone. "Pull up the weather on that thing."

He was happy to oblige. A few taps on his cell phone and the weather forecast showed clear for the next two days.

She frowned at the screen. "It's no good just getting it out of the house. We need it cleared away so Fran can do her business. Should we get a trailer?"

"Or a big rental truck! That would be great."

"Seth, may I remind you that your license is only good with me in the front seat. There's no way you're going to be able to drive the pickup alone hundreds of miles to Fresno."

He grinned. "I could drive the truck?"

"No. We need a covered trailer. One big enough to haul all this stuff. And we need to get it now. Can you look up trailer rental places?"

"Can do." He started tapping away as they got into the pickup.

There were a surprisingly large number of places that advertised trailers in this little city. He gave her directions and they drove over to Highway 101. They were pulling into a self-storage place that also had trailer's for rent when her phone rang.

She hurriedly pulled into a parking space and answered. "Hello?"

Seth hopped out and started wandering around the lot, looking at the various sizes of the trailers. They had a hitch on the pickup already, so that wasn't a problem, but they'd need a trailer big enough to handle all the stuff from the house.

What did people do before these trailer places went nationwide so you could rent them one-way? Make a second trip to bring it back, or just buy a trailer and sell it when you got to your destination?

He wanted to get one big enough. He'd been worrying about their luggage. On the trip up, they had camped at a roadside rest area in sleeping bags. If they filled up the pickup storage area, then they would need to stay at a motel, and that cost more money. It might be possible to make the whole drive in one day, but that hadn't worked coming up. They were always late getting started. It might have been better if she let him drive while she rested, but he couldn't get that obvious piece of wisdom through her head.

He looked back at the pickup. Biz hadn't gotten out. He hoped it wasn't a call from the realtor pushing up the deadline.

Her head was down, resting on the steering wheel. He started walking faster.

"Sis?"

She looked up and her eyes were all messy from tears.

"What's wrong?"

"That was work. They laid me off."

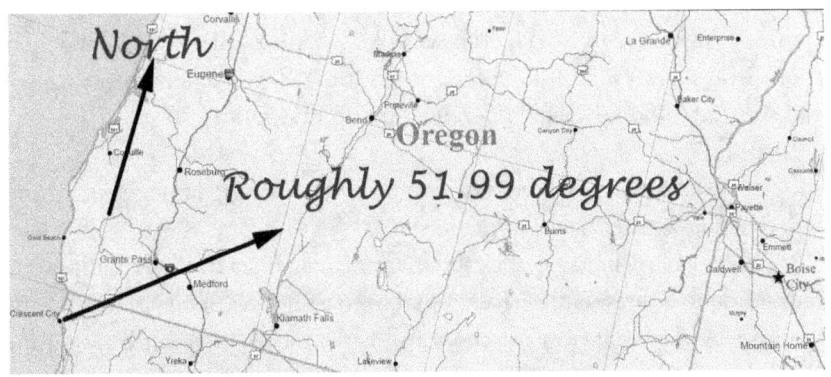

North

Oregon

Roughly 51.99 degrees

Chapter 3: Road Trip

"What happened?"

She rubbed her eyes. "I don't know. I knew there was a layoff in the wind, but they told me that taking this trip wouldn't put me at risk. This was vacation time! I asked off months ago."

Seth was at a loss. What could he say? Biz had always been on top of the day to day stuff, making a living and paying the bills. He wasn't really sure what this news meant to them.

"Uh, what do we do now?"

She took a deep breath. "Officially, I'm supposed to check back in three months. But until then, there's no job."

"And no paycheck?"

"No paycheck, sort of. They said they would deposit my last paycheck and pay me for all my vacation time, but nothing until, and if, the job opens back up in September."

"So it could be longer than three months?"

She shrugged. "I'm going to have to get another job to hold us as it is." Suddenly, she honked the horn for five long seconds. "I hate this!"

Her eyes were starting to water again. He patted her on the back. It was awkward, but it was the best he could do standing beside her through the open window.

"Did your boss say anything more?"

"It wasn't Jess. It was his boss, Mr. Boyer, who called me. He was all sympathetic-voice and saying all the nice comfort phrases they probably trained him to use in managerial school. But it was all a script. He had a short little answer for all the standard questions. It was a 'temporary financial shortfall' and it 'wasn't any reflection on my work'.

"Bull!"

Seth was a little shocked. Biz never used any strong language, and the fact that she went that far said volumes.

Biz had been holding their little family together by sheer willpower. Her solid job at Fresnel Electronics had been a big part of her ability to pull it all off. And it kept him in school full time, rather than out hunting for odd jobs as well.

I wish Momma or Dad were still here. They would have some words of wisdom to add. He had to say something, anything.

"But we have savings. And the house will sell soon, right?"

She nodded, not meeting his eyes, just staring at the steering wheel in her hands. "Yes. And we have to keep going. We can't let this delay us from emptying out the house." She spoke like she was describing how to unclog a toilet. "Let's get this done, and then I can go back and start looking for another job."

Seth looked up as a workman came out of the office building, probably to see what the honking noise was about. He walked past the row of self storage buildings.

Self storage buildings!

"Maybe...maybe we don't have to go right back to Fresno." An idea started to sprout in his head.

"What do you mean?"

"Biz, maybe this isn't the end of the world." He tasted the idea, trying to phrase it carefully. He had to be cautious. He could spoil it all with a wrong word.

"You've got three months before you need to go back to your company. I've got plenty of time before school starts. Your layoff just means our deadline to get back home has been lifted. Yes, we need to empty out the house, but why don't we just rent one of these storage buildings for a month. Let's stash the stuff for now and treat ourselves to a vacation. A real one, like when we were little. We could follow that mystery 51.99 bearing on the cylinder and see where it leads us. Or we could go visit some of our old places. See the old vacation spots again. Remember how great that clam chowder tasted when we went to Portland the first time?" He was making it up as he talked, but when she showed just a flicker of interest, he kept it up. He'd been through enough grief counseling lately that he knew he had to get her mind on other things, at least for a little while.

Their parents had enjoyed traveling and as a family, they had gone to Yellowstone and Seattle and several other trips before Biz had gotten too involved with high school events and later with her college.

"That's not being responsible, Seth. We have some savings, that's true, but going too long without a job is just inviting disaster."

She sounded like Mom, when she had been worried.

"No. Your phone call came at exactly the right moment, before we rented the trailer. This change of schedule is a gift from God. You've been responsible enough for the both of us and you need to take a break. Don't argue with fate."

It was the same argument Dad often used when he had to dislodge practical Mom from her routine, and Biz smiled just a moment.

The rental guy walked up. "Do you need something?"

Biz looked up. Seth beamed at her hopefully.

She sighed. "I guess we need to rent a storage building."

...

SethPartner	Change of plans! We're going to find out where the cylinder came from.
nickyWhy	@SethPartner How are you gonna do that?

|  SethPartner | @nickyWhy Road trip! The cylinder has a GPS thingy that points off towards somewhere. We'll go that way. |

...

The camper shell came off easily and they were able to move all the furniture and boxes from the house to the storage building in three trips. They kept some pillows and bedding. One of the mattresses fit nicely into the pickup bed. The sleeping bags had been fine for the trip up, but they hadn't really planned for an extensive campout. The metal ribs of the pickup bed made for an uncomfortable sleep. Any cushioning would be useful.

After the last run, and after they'd put the camper shell back on, they had one last stop to make.

"I have to drop the keys off at Fran's office. I'll probably have some papers to sign before we can leave. Do you want to come in for that?"

"No, can you drop me over by the lighthouse. I want to take a couple of pictures with my phone."

...

|  moosenine | @SethPartner I told Sara you were crazy. Now I know it. |
|  SethPartner | @moosenine Road trip is a great idea. I'll never get Biz to do it otherwise. |

SethPartner	@moosenine BTW, who's Sara?
nickyWhy	@SethPartner @SaraCme is Moose's latest gf.

Seth clicked the new name tag and added it to his follow list.

SaraCme	@SethPartner Greetings Seth!
moosenine	Hey, I don't got no gf. I plsy the field.
SethPartner	@moosenine http://twitpic.com/zecbe here's my gf! 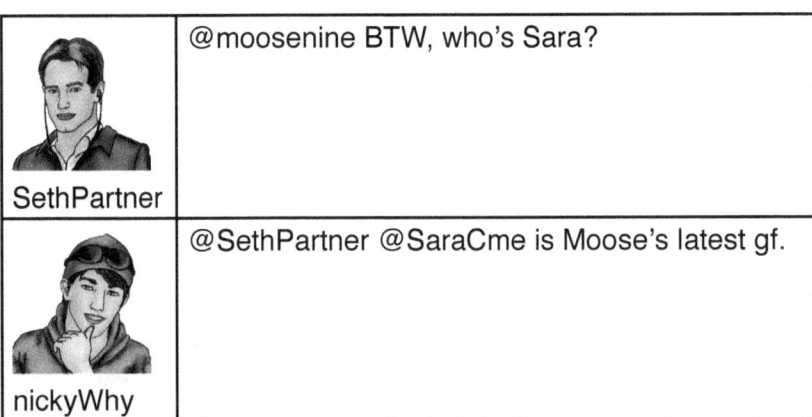
nickyWhy	@SethPartner That's your speed, Seth. Who's she?

	@nickyWhy I dunno. Just a carved statue here at the harbor. Saying my goodbyes to Crescent City.
SethPartner	

...

It was an hour later that Biz drove up to Citizens Dock in the pickup. She had been looking for him. He had managed to walk all the way down the harbor. For once he didn't mind that they had signed up for that service that let them track each other's phones. Her phone wasn't as capable as his, but it could at least locate him in a pinch. It was harder to hide from her, but it also meant he didn't have to keep her constantly updated on his location.

"You done here?" she asked as she walked up.

He took another look at a seal swimming into the inner harbor and nodded. Surely he'd be back some day. She followed his gaze and smiled a little sadly.

"Yeah. I'm hungry."

They hit the Burger King and then headed north out of town on US 199, the road that headed closest to a 52 degree bearing.

"I called Aunt Ally."

Seth raised an eyebrow. "Why?"

Biz sighed. "Someone has to take care of the house while we're gone. I asked her to house sit. She can get the mail and water the grass. Make it look lived in."

"You remember the last time she came to crash?"

"Yes, but she's been doing better lately, honest."

Seth reserved judgment. If Biz was 100 on the responsibility scale, he was at least a 60. Aunt Ally was about a 30. He hoped she wouldn't burn the place down.

...

"I can drive." Not too many miles down the road, surrounded by mountains and hedged in by endless dark green forest, Seth had no cell signal and with his phone connected to the charger, he felt at loose ends.

Biz was enjoying the curvy mountain Redwood Highway. She breathed in the evergreen-scented air. "Maybe later." Living in a desert valley, driving the forests was obviously soothing to her. He was jealous, but chose not to nag about it. Not yet.

Seth had stashed the cylinder where he could reach it from the front seat. He twisted off the protective end cap.

"The number has changed."

"Oh good. That means the GPS is still working. What's it read?"

"Hmm. 52.11. I guess that's just a decimal degree reading?"

"Probably, and it hasn't changed all that much."

"What does that mean?"

"Probably it means that we're still heading in the right direction, or else I guess it could mean that we are very far away from the destination point. It's like we're trying to find the North Pole by using a compass. If we're close, then the needle would swing around with every step, but if we're a thousand miles away, it wouldn't change very fast as we move. And a high altitude balloon could have traveled a long way."

"You still think that's where it came from?" He still reserved judgment.

"Your guess is as good as mine, but you're right, there're no fins or rocket motor or anything like that. And it did fall out of the sky."

There didn't appear to be any kind of cable hook either, and that nagged at him. If it had been carried by a balloon, how was it attached?

...

"Grant Pass, Oregon, and the gadget reads 52.75."

Biz frowned, "That still less than a degree of change and we've gone quite a distance. I guess we're on the right track, but we have to join I-5 just up ahead. Let me see a map."

She pulled to the shoulder and they unfolded the California highway map. "We're going to need a new one, or maybe an atlas." But there was just enough overlap into Oregon to show what happened at Grant Pass.

Seth gestured with his hand. "Zero would be north, and 90 degrees would be straight east. I guess we need to go sort of this way."

Unfortunately the highway wasn't going to co-operate. north or southeast were the only choices. She tapped the map. "We'll go north for now. Watch the GPS reading and we'll find an eastward highway when we need it."

SethPartner	Back on the interstate in Oregon. Heading north. Got signal for now.
ClaraN1	@SethPartner Is it pretty there?
SethPartner	@claraN1 Yes, but there's cities and stuff where I am now. It's not like forests and oceans. I'm already missing CC.
moosenine	@SethPartner North? It's gonna take forever to get you back here. Game's getting pretty stale.
SethPartner	@moosenine Clara not up to the job?
ClaraN1	@SethPartner Watch it there! Moose is just sore I fragged him good last night.

moosenine	U wish.
SethPartner	Can Sara play?
SaraCme	@SethPartner they asked, but I don't have the game. It's Barstow, and they're out.
SethPartner	Oops. L8tr. Biz is letting me drive. FTW!

...

The traffic started to bunch up a little as they approached Salem, Oregon. Seth had been feeling confident after driving a few dozen miles in the stable and comfortable interstate lanes, but he frowned at the curved and ancient little car poking along in his lane. A quick look at the mirrors and he jerked the wheel and changed lanes. Ahh! He added some gas and passed the old Volkswagen and quickly caught up with the shiny gasoline transport truck. There was room, so he changed lanes again and moved on.

Biz chuckled.

"What?" He risked a look at her face. She was laughing at him.

"Oh, nothing. You just drive like Mom did."

"What do you mean?"

"Nothing. Just pay attention to the road and stay within the speed limits. We can't afford a ticket right now."

"No. Tell me what you mean."

She hesitated. He had to keep his eyes on the road, so he couldn't tell what she was thinking about.

But soon, she said, "Back when I was learning to drive, Dad was still in town, so I got driving lessons from the both of them."

Seth felt a little twinge of jealousy.

"One thing I noticed was that they drove with completely different styles. Dad was a planner. If there was an exit ten miles ahead, he'd move to the correct lane and never need to change it. Mom would shift lanes like a butterfly, moving back and forth on a whim. I was always terrified as we'd get close to our turn and she'd need to cross several lanes in the last hundred yards. She always made it, but I was never that brave."

...

Entering Portland, Biz picked up the cylinder and frowned at it.

"What's the number?"

She said, "55.97, but I don't like this looks of this."

"What?"

He was blocked in by cars on both sides and kept his eyes on his mirrors. City traffic made him nervous.

"The digital display is flickering. I think maybe the batteries are getting weak. We can't risk letting the GPS go dead, even for a fraction of a second. With its control chip broken, we'd never get the reading back."

"What do we do?"

"Give me your phone. I need to find a Radio Shack."

He fished it out of his pocket and took the opportunity to move to the slow lane.

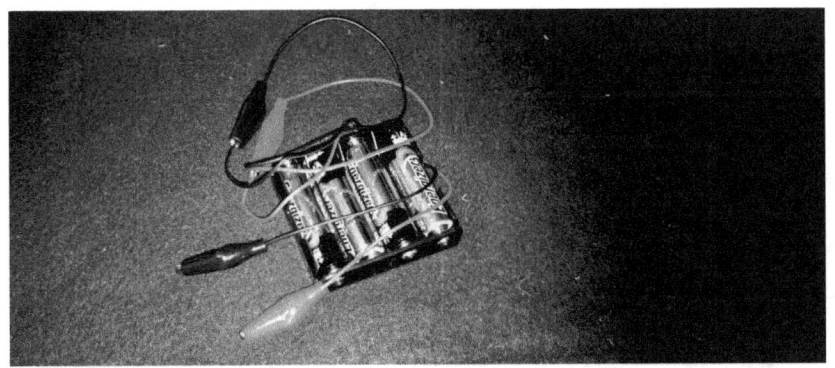

Chapter 4: Northward

When it came to electronics, Biz was all business. They found the Radio Shack. Seth was a little jittery from navigating the unfamiliar city traffic when they pulled into the parking lot, but she was out the door in a flash.

Shortly, she was back with a brick of AA batteries, an external battery pack and a bundle of alligator clip leads.

"The trick is to never let the voltage vanish." She added batteries to the external pack and then with the alligator clips, paralleled the external pack with the set that was in the cylinder. The numbers got noticeably blacker as the fresh batteries raised the voltage.

"Now, we can replace the old ones." She put action to words and he collected the exhausted cells.

He held one close enough to read. "Hey, these have French writing on them. The label is bilingual."

She finished up by removing the external battery pack.

"Why don't you just leave that connected?"

"Don't parallel batteries unless you have to. If they have different charges, then the strong one will try to charge the weak one and unless they're rechargables designed for that, you can cause trouble. We'll just pay better attention to the charge. I bought plenty of extra batteries." She patted the large package. "But let me see those."

She read the label on the old batteries. "Probably from Canada. We need an atlas."

They drove around and found a Walmart. She had a new atlas and a drawing protractor. "I should have written down the readings. It was 51.99 back in Crescent City, right?"

He nodded. She drew a line from the coast of California just south of Oregon at 52 degrees on the big overview map. Then she marked Portland and drew one at 56 degrees. The lines crossed somewhere in Eastern Canada.

She sighed. "That's a long, long way from here. I know the lines aren't accurate, but the GPS has to be pointing towards some place near there. Do we really want to go all that way?"

"How long would it take?"

"I don't know. A week or two—just as long to get back."

"They said you were free for three months. School doesn't start for two months. You know, we'll never get another chance to take a trip like this ever again in our lives. You'll be working. I'll be in college before you realize it. Look at this map. We could visit Yellowstone, the Great Lakes, big stretches of Canada that we've never seen. I'll risk three or four weeks for that."

"It'll cost a lot of gas."

He laughed. "It'll be worth it. Besides...Canada! You've said you always wanted to see an aurora. This might be your chance."

"I can't commit to the whole thing. We can do Yellowstone, but you'd talk me into an around the world tour if the pickup could drive across the water."

"One day at a time, then." He didn't deny it.

She nodded. They got on Interstate 84 and headed east.

...

nickyWhy	Two days in Yellowstone? Whatever happened to your quest for the secret gadget?

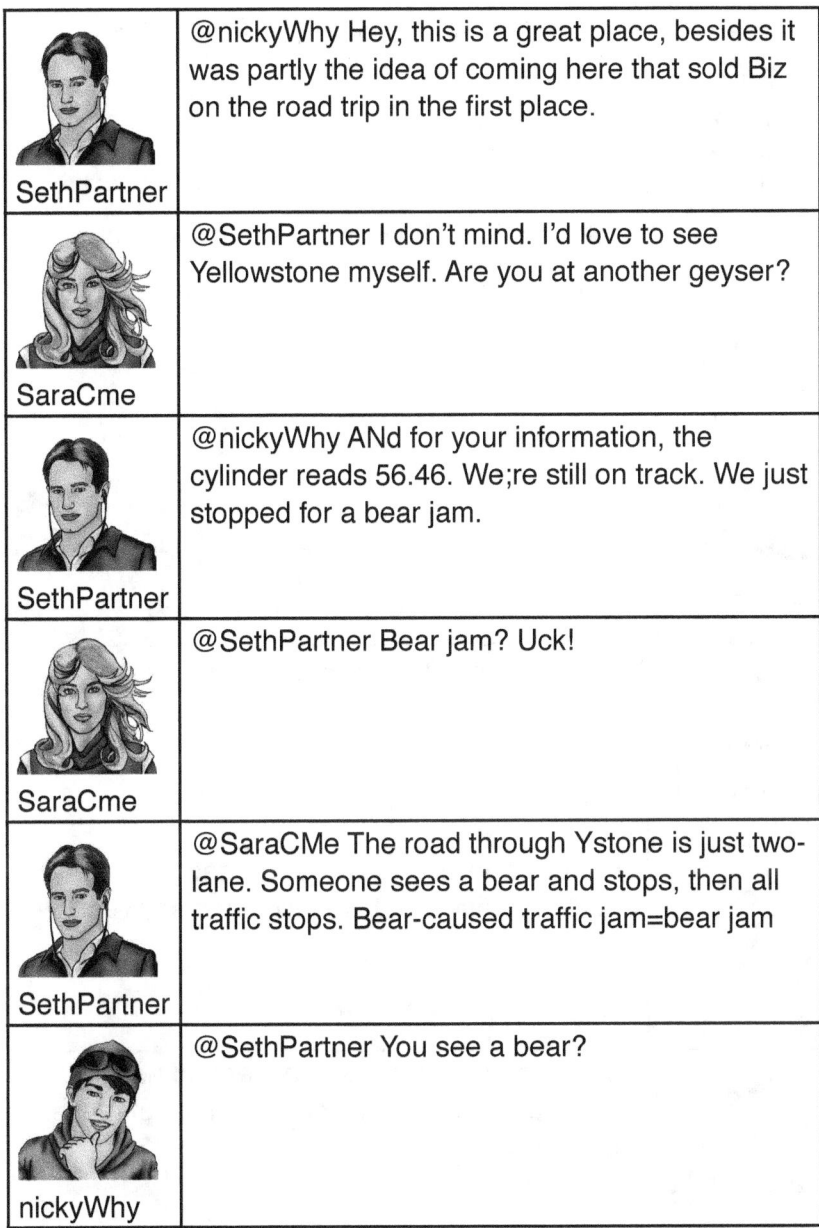

SethPartner	@nickyWhy Hey, this is a great place, besides it was partly the idea of coming here that sold Biz on the road trip in the first place.
SaraCme	@SethPartner I don't mind. I'd love to see Yellowstone myself. Are you at another geyser?
SethPartner	@nickyWhy ANd for your information, the cylinder reads 56.46. We;re still on track. We just stopped for a bear jam.
SaraCme	@SethPartner Bear jam? Uck!
SethPartner	@SaraCMe The road through Ystone is just two-lane. Someone sees a bear and stops, then all traffic stops. Bear-caused traffic jam=bear jam
nickyWhy	@SethPartner You see a bear?

SethPartner	@nickyWhy Yeah, a grizzly. Hang on. Pic http://twitpic.com/zlcbs
SaraCme	@SethPartner Oh! How cute! She has cubs.
SethPartner	@SaraCMe Here's a shot I took yesterday. Buffalo jam http://twitpic.com/zldzz
moosenine	@SethPartner You see any moose?
SethPartner	@moosenine No moose. Supposed to be here, and I'm looking, but I haven't found any yet.
SethPartner	Biz is heading back. Park ranger had her corralled with others to keep them out of range of the bear. l8tr

...

Biz was flushed and breathless as she rushed up and hopped into the cab.

"Did you get a good picture?"

She beamed, "Yes, and one of the professional photographers let me get a close up look through her huge telephoto lens. But I bet you got a good view, when she crossed the road, she came right beside the pickup. I'd have done better to stay inside."

Seth showed off his snap.

"Are you glad we came?"

She started the engine. "Oh yes!"

"You know, we're really close to Montana. There's no need to turn back yet."

She gave him a familiar look. "I expected you to say something like that." But she didn't say no.

...

The next day, on Interstate 90, the distinctive chime of her cell phone was just barely loud enough to be heard over the road noise.

She looked at the screen carefully while driving. She frowned. "I've got a text. We're approaching Chamberlain, South Dakota. I need to stop and make a call."

Seth felt a sinking feeling. He had just convinced her to stretch their trip as far as the Great Lakes. A phone call could only come from back in California–something to drag them back home.

They pulled off at a likely exit near the Missouri River and found a place to stop at a city park next to the water. She walked over to a picnic table with her phone.

Seth pulled out the cylinder and checked the reading. 54.58, the numbers kept changing, but it never seemed like they were making any progress. He had mixed feelings about that. If they stayed on course, then they weren't wasting gas heading off on side trips.

Not that he minded the idea of side trips, but it would be a good idea to finally discover what the gadget was and where it came from.

They stopped each night when they found a place to park the pickup at a relatively safe place. That was usually a highway rest area, or like in Yellowstone, an official camp ground. But once they camped, there was no

TV, no games other than solitaire on her laptop and game apps on his cell phone. Often he went to bed before he was really tired and there was lots of time to think about the cylinder.

He was less convinced it was a balloon instrument package than Biz was. For one thing, there were no rings or brackets or any place to secure it to a balloon. You wouldn't send one of those up with it just resting loose in a basket.

There was also no sign of the balloon. Sure, it could have blown out over the Pacific and been lost, but there'd been nothing on the net about a balloon. He'd only had a limited time on the laptop, and it had been a welcome find to see all the Wi-Fi hotspots at the state highway rest stops, but he'd had to ask the gang to do more elaborate searches for him. Nick and Sara gave him some hits, but there was nothing that seemed to match what had struck his tree.

The undamaged part of the cylinder was smooth and even streamlined, as if it had been intended to fall through the sky. Before they left Crescent City, he'd considered a detachable payload from a rocket launch, or even fired from a cannon, but here they were long past California, beyond Yellowstone, beyond Mt. Rushmore, something like 2000 road miles away from where it had crashed, and there was still no sign they were close.

Governments could fire rockets like that, but didn't they mark their stuff with something more useful than a cryptic string of numbers?

He sighed. Of course, having no solution yet was helping him convince Biz to keep traveling. It puzzled her, too, and the hacked electronics was just her kind of mystery.

A glance over at the picnic table showed Biz earnestly talking to someone. He hoped it wasn't more bad news. Yesterday she'd called Fran about the house, but it seemed the paperwork of real estate goes on forever. Sooner or later, they'd have to find a way to fax the final signed documents back to the realtor to finish out the sale.

His sister lowered her phone. As she walked back, he saw bad signs. Biz was furious. Her face was tight and her eyes stared hard at the sidewalk about ten feet in front of her.

"What's up?"

She just shook her head and started the engine. Heading out of town, he decided not to mention the food places they were passing by. She was intent on getting back on the interstate.

Back on I-90, Seth eyed the speedometer from his side of the cab. She was pushing the speed limit past where she was usually comfortable. Something bad had happened, but they were still heading away from home.

Before long they were nearing Sioux Falls and her cell phone chimed again. She ignored it and took the cloverleaf and headed north on Interstate 29. Seth's stomach growled, but he put it on hold.

He fished out his phone and fingered the tiny keyboard.

SethPartner	Biz is upset about something. Driving like a maniac--for her. Not talking.
SaraCme	@SethPartner She's there with you, ask her.
ClaraN1	@SaraCMe I dunno. I met Biz in RL. Nice lady but not chatty. Seth, I'd just be patient until she's ready.

He agreed. Time to wait it out.

...

The pickup drifted into the rumble strips.

"Hey Sis. Do you want me to drive?"

She nodded, reluctantly, and pulled off on the shoulder. They raided the ice chest to make sandwiches while trucks whooshed by just a few feet away. The pickup shook from the wind each time.

Seth gobbled down his sandwich and set his drink into the cup-holder.

"We're driving north?"

"Yes. Let's get into Canada as soon as possible."

She was still upset, not meeting his eyes. He took a quick glance at the map.

...

In the dwindling twilight, a red Corvette zipped past and he added a little gas.

Oh, that's a car I'd like to have. It was certainly more likely to catch a girl's eye than a Buick. *And I bet it takes off like a rocket when you stomp the throttle.*

Biz was asleep, and it seemed he had clear permission to push past the speed limit. Just a few days ago, when he'd asked about Dad's words of wisdom about driving, she had tried to pass on what he'd said.

"'There are three speed limits', Dad said. 'The posted limit, the safe limit, and the comfort limit.'"

Biz explained what he meant. The posted limit on the sign was obvious. The safe limit was the real limit dependent on the car, the road, the traffic and the weather. Exceed the safe limit and you're likely to crash.

"The comfort limit is what you drive when you're not even thinking about speed. It's what you drive when you're on auto-pilot. Most speeding tickets happen when the comfort limit exceeds the posted limit."

Seth let the Corvette get far ahead, nearly a half-mile, close enough so he could see the first blink of tail lights if it should see a radar trap or a road hazard.

Biz had said, "If you need to exceed the posted limit, never exceed the safe limit, and only push the comfort limit when you have an emergency. If at all possible, wait to follow someone who passes you. Let them take the risk of a traffic ticket. And if you do get a ticket, be polite and don't argue with the police. It was your decision and you have to accept the penalty."

The Corvette was far enough ahead, and Seth had to push harder to keep it from pulling away. The speedometer was 90 and climbing. How fast was he going?

Their pickup was handling the speed, but just barely. The engine was loud and the suspension had a little vibration in it. He had a touch of regret at leaving the panel truck behind that he had been pacing at 78. *I can handle the speed, but this junker we drive can't.*

In the weeks after Mom died, they were tight for cash, juggling funeral expenses, legal bills. It had been hard enough just trying to settle into a new way of living. Selling the Suburban had given them needed funds, but it made the chances of getting his own ride much more difficult. He might have to get a new job himself to buy one, although he didn't look forward to restarting that fight. Biz wanted him concentrating on school, with plans for him to get a scholarship. *As if my GPA is good enough for that to happen.*

The tail lights far up ahead flashed, for just an instant, and Seth let off the gas. But the Corvette must have kept going, because it again started to dwindle in size. He put more pressure on the throttle. It wasn't a speed trap after all.

Quickly, he covered the distance. To his right, there was a flicker of motion. Before he could even think to act, three deer dashed across the road. Two crossed in front of him. One held off.

For three heartbeats, he just kept cruising. Blind luck had kept those deer from committing suicide-by-car, and demolishing the pickup and both of them in the process.

I'm going too fast. It was now definitely faster than his personal comfort limit. Reluctantly, he snapped the imaginary tow-rope and let the red car vanish in the distance. He drifted back down to the posted limit. It was fast enough, for now.

...

Approaching the I-94 cloverleaf, he asked, "Still north?"

He hadn't mentioned the deer, and maybe he wouldn't. It certainly wouldn't help her perception of his driving skills.

She blinked and straightened up in her seat. She nodded. "On to Canada. I want to get out of cell phone range."

He didn't question. Biz was being impulsive, he got that. But she was stable. More stable than he was. She had her reasons. According to Rule Five, he could always question her decisions, but that could wait until she had calmed down.

It was tough to hold off, but he would *not* be the needy little kid brother! They were partners, and if now was the time he needed to take care of her, then so be it.

...

A few miles shy of the border, he made a decision to pull into a road-side rest area. It had a bathroom and he didn't know if you could cross the border at night or not.

Biz just nodded at his explanation, made use of the facilities and climbed into the back to sleep. He grabbed blankets and a couple of pillows and stretched out in the cab.

...

	We'll be in Canada, starting tomorrow. I have a bad feeling I won't be able to tweet much.
SethPartner	

His friends chatted away, but before too many words had scrolled off the screen, he was asleep. He dreamed of deer in the headlights.

Chapter 5: Canada

"Are you here for business or pleasure?"

Biz handed the Canadian border guard, dressed with a bullet-proof vest over her uniform, their passports. Biz had gotten hers when it seemed possible she might be doing some travel for her company and Seth had demanded she get one for him, too. It was just luck that she had them in her travel case.

Seth thought the guard looked cute in her uniform, and would have tweeted so, except Biz had warned him to shut down his phone. They were entering Canadian cell phone territory and international roaming charges were severe.

There were a few other questions. They drove over to another building and another border guard had them step out while he searched the pickup.

Biz pointed over to the lane where truckers were answering their own questions. "Look, every time a new vehicle stops, those two birds move in and eat the insects off the radiator grill." That truck moved on, and the next one stopped. Just as she'd noticed, the birds swooped in and feasted on bugs they didn't have to chase.

He would have tweeted about that as well.

The border guard rummaged around in their camping gear and then told them they were free to pass. Only when Seth got back in the cab did he notice the cylinder sitting in the floor.

As they drove out, he picked it up. "I guess they didn't notice this. What would you have said if they asked about it?"

She chuckled. "I have no idea. Do you think they thought it was a thermos? I guess it would look suspicious, now that you mention it. Oh well, we won't be crossing the border again until we head back home. We'll worry about it then."

Seth was glad she was cheerier this morning.

Biz pointed at the tourist building. "We need to stop there and pick up some Canadian cash. Do you have any money you need to convert?"

"Not likely. Just loose change."

"Well, stash it away so you won't accidentally try to use it."

"I wonder if they have Wi-Fi. If I can't use my phone network, I can at least connect that way."

"Winnipeg is just a ways up the road. It's a big city. We'll stop at a place with free Wi-Fi and eat."

...

SethPartner	I was right. My phone net is shut down for as long as we're in Canada. I'll only be able to tweet when we find wifi.
SaraCme	@SethPartner Be sure and let me know where you're at and post pictures. I'm following your trip with markers on Google Earth.
nickyWhy	@SethPartner You should be able to get international service. Check phone co's website.

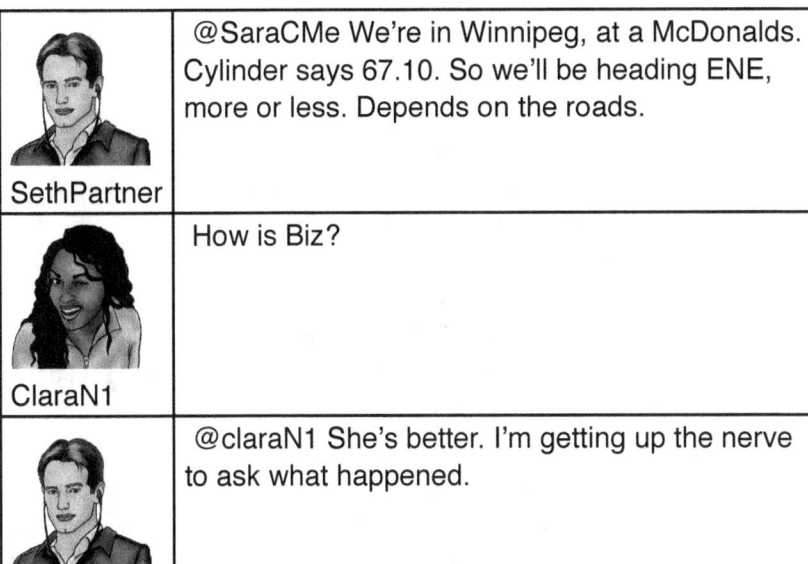

SethPartner	@SaraCMe We're in Winnipeg, at a McDonalds. Cylinder says 67.10. So we'll be heading ENE, more or less. Depends on the roads.
ClaraN1	How is Biz?
SethPartner	@claraN1 She's better. I'm getting up the nerve to ask what happened.

...

Seth set down his phone and reached for a napkin to wipe mayonnaise off his face. "Okay Biz. Why did we make a dash for Canada after your phone call?"

She had been looking over the maps. The Walmart road atlas had Canadian coverage, but not at any detail.

"Oh, I'd just gotten interested in where the GPS is pointing, aren't you? We've still got to cross the bulk of the country and it looks like most of the good roads are in the southern part, close to the border."

"Rule Five, Biz. You said head north and I didn't object. But I want to know why."

She looked away and said nothing for nearly a minute. It was really hard for them to lie to each other, after all they'd been through. He just sat and waited.

"There was a text message that said to call Jess Freeman."

"Your boss at Fresnel."

"Right. So I stopped and called him. I figured he might have more details about the layoff."

"Did he?"

Her face twisted, as if she'd eaten something disgusting. "I liked Jess, as a boss. He wasn't that much older than me, and listened when I had things to contribute. He worked to help me get the time off to sell the house. I really thought he was on my side."

Seth just waited. She was struggling to get the words out.

"When I called him...he was happy with the layoff! It 'removed the barriers'. If he wasn't my boss and I wasn't his employee, then we could date!"

"Oh." Suddenly things made sense.

She was getting angry again, but at least she was talking. "He just doesn't get it. Doesn't he know I can't ever come back to work there now? From now on, it would always be awkward. He's ruined my job. He may have even sabotaged it, for all I know. I can never trust him again."

The map in her hand was getting wrinkled from her grip on it. He gently tugged it away from her.

She looked him in the eyes. Hers were shiny.

"What really, really tore me up was that I had to say nothing! There I was, in the park, discovering that my job had just been torn into shreds by this...clueless, idiot, and I had to *hide* what I felt about it."

"Why? Just tell him off."

She shook her head. "No. This was my first real job out of school. Every new job is going to want to know what kind of employee I have been. Jess is going to be the person they call when I apply for a new job. He's my reference! I can't leave with bad feelings to cloud that."

"Sue for sexual harassment."

"Tempting, but no. He really is just a clueless idiot. Maybe after I find a good new job elsewhere, I'll drop a note to his boss, Boyer, and wise him up, but stirring up a legal storm wouldn't get me a good job and might not even stick. That's just a recipe for making enemies.

"No, I have to stay quiet about this whole mess and write off Fresnel Electronics as just valuable job experience. I'm good. I can get another job.

"But anyway," she took another deep breath and tried to clear it out of her mind, "I told Jess we were heading into Canada and wouldn't have cell phone coverage for a few days. I wanted to make that true. I can ignore email easy enough and turn off all the chat options on my laptop.

"You need to stay quiet about this too. Understand? No stink on the Internet."

Seth nodded, but that wouldn't be easy.

"So, now, I need your opinion on our route out of here. We can take the Trans Canada Highway directly east, or go up this way to Lake Winnipeg and take this waterway route back down."

...

SethPartner	Quick report from Thunder Bay. We went up to Lk Winnipeg, down a waterway with lots and lots of hydro electric plants.
SaraCme	@SethPartner Which waterway? GE shows a zillion of them.
SethPartner	@SaraCMe Didn't catch the name. There was a 'Great Falls Power Plant' with a dried up 'Great Falls'. All goes through the turbines now.
moosenine	See any moose?

SethPartner	@moosenine No moose yet. I'll let you know.
ClaraN1	@SethPartner How is your sister?
SethPartner	@claraN1 She's fine. Just upset about losing her job.
nickyWhy	@SethPartner So....you're officially bums now?
SethPartner	@nickyWhy Let's just say, 'Currently without employer.'
nickyWhy	@SethPartner cool. If my parents lost their job, they'd be drinking the cyanide. You're just travel'n the world. My hero.

"Hey, Biz, take a look at this." He held out his phone.

She looked, and sighed. "Remind me how cool it is when we have to sell your phone to pay for groceries."

Their food arrived. They had stopped at an old railroad station next to the Thunder Bay harbor. It was a nice park area with lots of people walking on the sunny, but cool day. They had decided to splurge for a real meal with vegetables, salads and everything. Eating out of the ice chest was cheapest, but it could get boring.

Seth looked out over the bay, seeing islands and peninsulas in the far distance. They had made it to the Great Lakes after all. He hadn't expected to see them from the Canadian side first.

"So this is Lake Superior?"

"Thunder Bay on Lake Superior."

"I bet it does."

"What?"

"Thunder. See those mountains. When a thunderstorm comes through here, I can imagine the rumble would roll across the bay. Maybe, somebody came up with that name, and other people went along with it. That's my theory."

...

"How's our GPS number?"

They dug it out. "Uh-oh. The digits are fading again."

Hurriedly, Biz did the battery changing operation again.

"62.56. Anything less than 90 means we still need to go north, but all the good highways, according to the map, are south, close to the United States."

Seth looked over her shoulder. The Canadian parts of the atlas were colored differently and showed much less detail than the areas on the other side of the lakes. They needed a real Canadian map rather than a USA-based one.

"Is there a road up to Hudson's Bay? We're pretty close. That would be cool."

They searched the atlas, but saw nothing.

"There may be one, but if so, it's too small to show up on this map. But we can take this Highway 11 route across. As long as there are gas stations. There has to be. Should we buy a gas can? I don't know. Let's just keep the tank topped up every chance we get."

He admitted to some uncertainty as well. There ought to be gas stations, food stops, motels, etc. for the locals if for no other reason. But the truth was that they were in a different country and their guesses were just that, guesses.

...

Everything went smoothly until the day they crossed over into Québec. Suddenly all the road signs changed.

Seth had been looking forward to crossing the provincial border into French-speaking Québec, particularly for the road signs. Every time they saw a sign in both English and French, the French version took more words, and longer words, than the English version. It was his theory that it was just because English people were doing the translation and that when the French speakers did their signs, the imbalance would reverse and he'd be reading silly awkward English.

But those crafty Québec people had elected to use symbolic signs to get around any need for English at all. The stop signs were red octagonals like normal, but with no word in the middle. 'Slippery when wet' and 'watch for falling rocks' all had little cartoons illustrating the condition. The problem was that some of them weren't obvious. He had to puzzle over a sign several times before he figured out what they meant to say.

Biz looked embarrassed as she struggled at the gas station. "There's no pay-at-the-pump and people here don't need to speak English, so they don't. I just have to get by pointing and nodding." She was frustrated. "I always thought I could get by with my high school French, but I'm blowing it. I had friends who'd gone to Paris and had no trouble. It's different here. At least there are gas stations. I'll just make sure to fill up at every town."

They stopped at a restaurant that accentuated the language problem. Seth smiled and pointed at something on a wall poster while Biz struggled to read from the menu. But the locals couldn't understand her. No signs were in English, but at least 'motel' seemed to be a dual purpose word. And they had Wi-Fi.

...

Seth tried to catch up with his friends via tweets. He gushed about the scenery, they talked movies. It occurred to Seth that he hadn't seen a movie in days. The towns up here in the northern part of Québec were too small to support anything as grandiose as a multiplex, and he hadn't seen any signs that said "cinema" or anything like that. In some ways, he didn't have much to talk about. He certainly wasn't going to talk about family problems. He updated Sara on his location and after a bit he walked outside and tried to look for an aurora. The night time sky was disappointing. The town had orange street lights everywhere and even stars were hard to see. Biz was on her laptop, doing a job search for places back in California. He wondered if she were really interested in their quest across Canada to the mystery spot, or if the trip was just a temporary excuse to hide from a life that had turned upside down.

A couple passed by on the sidewalk. They were chatting, and the girl laughed. But, it was all totally unintelligible.

Back in Fresno, he often heard conversations in Spanish, but growing up in that community, he knew "casa" and "mañana" and a couple of dozen other words—just enough to puzzle out what people were talking about. Now among the French-speaking population, it was the first time he'd really felt like an outsider. He never thought he'd be homesick for Fresno.

Am I running away from my problems like Biz is with her job? I like the travel, but unless we can solve the cylinder mystery, will it be worth the extra pressure on our budget? I can't let it all fall on Biz. I need a job myself. I need to be a full partner.

He turned back toward the motel. Maybe tomorrow would be better.

Chapter 6: Parlez-vous Anglais

They blasted through Montréal as fast as the traffic would let them. Seth didn't even offer to drive. It was almost surreal, this French speaking high density population, after days in the empty woods. He spent most of his time trying to make sense of the roadsigns. He knew that the highway heading towards Québec City was 138, but the roads weren't marked as well as he would prefer. Deep in the downtown area, Biz would have crossed over to the south side of the St. Lawrence if he hadn't warned her.

At least here in a city, there were a few familiar sights like the McDonalds. And it had Wi-Fi.

•••

SethPartner	I'm having Cheeseburger avec bacon with frites. I had to point to the menu, but I think I could gradually learn some french.
SethPartner	The McDonalds sign is a big yellow M like at home, except in the middle is a tiny little Canadian maple leaf.

nickyWhy	@SethPartner Do they have a quarter pounder?
SethPartner	@nickyWhy Watching too many movies Nick? I see a sign that shows a 'Sandwich Double Quart De Livre avec fromage'
SaraCme	Are you in Montreal?
SethPartner	@SaraCMe Down the road a ways, in a place called three rivers, only spelled in French.

...

Using the Internet, Biz discovered that there was a laundromat just across the street, once they realized that the name they needed to google was a "buanderie".

"We have to stop and do it now, no matter how long it takes. We didn't pack for a trip this long and I've been wearing these jeans so long they've begun to stink."

There was a change machine that took bills and spit out the loonies and twonies–one and two dollar coins–that the machines used. Biz attempted to talk to the older couple that ran the laundry, it was too much effort for him. He walked the two blocks over to see the water. It was residential, with houses right up to the water.

The St. Lawrence was a big river here. This was all the runoff from the huge Great Lakes, all through this passage. After Québec, there were no more bridges on the map, it would be too wide for that. The atlas showed ferry routes to get to the southern shore. After they located the mystery spot, would they come back this way, or take one of those ferries?

...

As they drove through the city of Québec, Biz marveled at the old architecture, especially the Château Frontenac rising high over the St. Lawrence.

"Why don't we just spend a couple of days here and check out the old churches and museums? We don't have anything this old in Fresno. Then we should really cross over to the southern shore and make our way back home."

Seth frowned. "Are you really ready to head back, before we've found the source of the cylinder?"

She turned at the light. "I'd like to, but I really ought to turn back and start looking for a new job. I need to be hunting for a real replacement job, not just something to hold me over until the layoff is done. This is a waste of valuable time, chasing thousands of miles..."

"Kilometers."

She smiled. "Yes, thousands of kilometers, for a place that may or may not exist."

"But wouldn't it bother you to turn back if when you were so close? I still haven't found a moose for Moose yet. People are counting on me."

"I'm not spending all this money on gas just to make your buddies happy!"

"No. I'd be doing this just for me. It's just more fun with a bunch of friends in my pocket."

The look on her face as she gave up trying to argue gave him a pang of sympathy. If he were feeling lonely, what must she be going through? As near as he had noticed, most of the people she hung out with were from work. If she were really planning to never return to her job, then that meant leaving behind her circle of friends as well.

If her only friend was a teenage brother, she was in a bad situation.

I've got to pay more attention to what she needs. My gang is great, but she's the only family I've got.

Other than Aunt Ally, but she didn't really count.

And he could tell that he'd better be ready with a good reason to stay on the quest. Hunting for a good job wasn't a trivial reason for going home. It was reasonable. And Fresno was thousands of miles away. It would take time just to get back there.

I wish I could travel for months on end. Sign up for cheap international roaming somewhere and just live out of the back of the pickup. It's not all that hard.

...

That night, in a motel on Highway 138, Biz received a fax on her laptop. She'd signed up with an electronic fax company and the contract for the house arrived as an enclosure. Struggling with software not really designed for the purpose, she initialed the PDF and used a drawing program to capture her signature and paste it in place before uploading it to the fax gateway.

He looked up as she gave a big sigh. "The deal is approved. In a few days, I'll have a few more forms to sign and then we'll have the money."

"Good. Come take a look at this."

He had gotten the latest bearing from the cylinder. "It's 31.88. It's really changing fast now that we're getting closer. Here's what it looks like on the map. He laid the ruler on the flattened map page. We're going to have to go north before long."

She frowned at his results and pointed to an erratic trace on the map. "There is a road that goes up that way, but it looks like nothing but wilderness. We can't afford to be out of contact, especially with the final documents left to sign."

"But we're really close! It can't be more than a couple of days away."

She tapped her fingers nervously on the table top. Finally, she sighed. "Okay, I'll agree to take this road up far enough to stick our feet in Labrador—just so we can say we've been there. If the mystery spot doesn't appear by then...well, we've given it a good shot. We can then turn around and head back home. Aren't you ready to get back to your friends?"

The question surprised him. They'd certainly flip-flopped on this trip. First he wanted to hunt for the source of the cylinder, and by the time he'd gotten a little bored with it, she was anxious to keep going.

Now that they were in strange territory where she couldn't even talk to anyone, she was ready to turn around.

But they were getting close, and he'd be happy to drive for as long as there was road under the wheels. And now it looked like she was ready to set a deadline. Rule Two. She was in charge and he'd exhausted his arguments.

"I guess so." His friends, his real friends, were all riding along with him, from hot-spot to hot-spot. Maybe he had his own reasons for staying away from Fresno for a while.

She nodded. "Let me call Aunt Ally while we still have phone service on the laptop."

Seth crossed his fingers while she fired up Skype.

Be sober. Be sober. A bad call could have them turning back tonight.

"Hello, Palmer residence."

"Hi Aunt Ally. I'm just checking in to see how things are going."

"Fine. Everything's fine."

"You've been getting the mail?"

"Ah, yeah. Just some junk and bills and stuff. Are you coming home?" She sounded a little worried.

"Oh, it'll be a few days yet."

"Ok then. Did you want anything?"

"Not yet. Just good to hear your voice."

"Yeah, you too. Bye." Click.

Seth chuckled, a little relieved. "She didn't even ask where we were."

Biz shook her head. "Don't laugh. She's family. And at least the house is still standing."

"Small blessings."

Ally Brooking was his mother's sister, and strictly speaking, the most likely person to become his guardian short of dropping him into the state care system. That she hadn't wanted anything to do with him, and that Biz had stepped up as a responsible adult had made all the difference.

"Biz?"

"Yes?"

"Thanks for being my guardian."

...

After Biz went to sleep, he settled down with her laptop, but after a couple of tries, he gave up trying to find someone on-line. Still, Internet access and a laptop were not resources to be wasted. Being on the road all the time left him far, far behind in his RSS feeds. There were a couple of thousand articles he hadn't been able to read. Before too long, they would expire.

World politics and the latest scandal bored him, so he prioritized the feeds. With no news anywhere about balloons, the cylinder had left him curious about space probes. The latest news from the NASA site was more followup on that solar panel accident on the ISS space station. The latest analysis of the impact had decided that it was a stray fragment from the Iridium accident that had struck the solar panel and caused all the damage. The space station had maneuvered to avoid a larger chunk from that same 2009 collision between the phone satellite and an old Russian Kosmos.

Everyone was grateful it hadn't struck the pressurized areas where the astronauts worked, but it meant more juggling of launch priorities to boost a replacement for the destroyed solar panel.

Just thinking about the International Space Station, and all that he'd read about it over the years made the idea that their backyard visitor was a space probe that much more ridiculous. He trusted Biz when it came to anything electronic and she said it was built with obsolete GPS parts and hacked on circuits. That yelled amateur, not the work of some government's space program.

One more twist in the mystery. Maybe the answers were up towards the northeast, hopefully on the road to Labrador.

...

They stopped at Baie-Comeau and ate burgers. The GPS was saying 29.76.

Biz was checking the maps they had picked up locally against the atlas, still marked with the bearing marks.

"We need to go inland, and this 'Labrador Highway' is the only way in. Are you up for it?"

"Of course."

"Let's get gas. And keep the tank filled. I don't see any towns anywhere close."

"Probably no Internet either. Can I find a place to update the Gang before we head in?"

They filled up, and Seth checked the tires and the oil. Biz was nervous about getting too far from civilization and he wanted to cover all the bases.

...

SethPartner	This may be my last check-in for a while. I'm at Baie-Comeau and we're heading north and I don't see any towns, so there may not be net.
nickyWhy	@SethPartner Will you have gas if there's no towns?
SethPartner	@nickyWhy I hope so. Nobody to ask (still French spkrs), and the locals drive it, so I have to trust there'll be gas.
SaraCme	@SethPartner Found the highway on my map. Goes up to Labrador City, then east. Lots of hydro electric plants.
SethPartner	@SaraCme Good. I'll tell Biz we have people watching over us. She worries.

moosenine	Find me a moose.
SethPartner	@moosenine Honest, I'm searching high & lo. Locals worry abt them all the time. See roadsign: http://twitpic.com/zx4ey
ClaraN1	@SethPartner Play it safe. Moose is sulking u been gone so long.

Chapter 7: Manic Cinq

Fingers crossed, they headed up the Labrador Highway.

"Look, there's traffic." It was a white pickup off in the distance. Otherwise, they had the road all to themselves. Ever present were the high voltage transmission towers.

"I love the names of these places," Biz pointed. The road sign marked how many kilometers to Manic 2, Manic 3 and Manic 5. When they passed the truck, it was marked with Hydro Québec.

"Biz, stop up there, I want to take a picture." She pulled off onto the shoulder and he stepped out. The air was buzzing, as well it should be. It was a huge field, maybe 50 acres, filled with transformers and giant insulators. Transmission lines came in from all directions. It was some kind of power hub.

"Those Manic places are all hydro electric power plants, I bet."

She nodded. "We saw those huge transmission lines coming this way from Québec and Montréal. I suspect they come from here. Canada has hydro plants all over the country."

Seth had thought those plants up by Winnipeg had been big, but by the looks of these transmission lines, the Manic plants must produce a lot more power. He wished he could send his picture to the gang, but this was really out in the middle of nowhere.

"I hope the gas stations aren't hidden away for the use of the power company vehicles only."

Biz nodded, "But I doubt we'll be stranded. This is a public highway. Somebody has to have thought this out."

...

Finally, after more than 200 kilometers in from the coast, after endless lakes and trees and no signs of civilization other than the transmission lines...gas pumps! It was quite a service stop, with a convenience store and rows of motel rooms.

Biz pulled in. "This is Manic 5, or Manic-Cinq as they call it." She pronounced it 'Manic-sank'. "Let's not push it any more today. Those rooms look appealing."

She went into the office. She came out beaming. "They gave us the 'VIP' rooms, and if I understood right, they have Internet."

Internet yes, but not wireless. There was an ethernet jack. Biz had it covered. From her tool kit, she produced the right cable and set her laptop to rebroadcast the net via Wi-Fi. They had their own private hotspot.

...

SethPartner	I'm really amazed to find net here. You don't understand just how far this is from 'civilization'. Manic-Cinq is like a little island.
SethPartner	Is anybody there?
SaraCme	@SethPartner They got a game going on, I gather. They invited me, but I don't have it. Got you marked on my map.

"Seth, I'm going to need to reboot. The net will drop."
"Give me a minute."

 **SethPartner**	@SaraCMe Looks like net problems here. l8tr

He put his phone on the charger. "What's up?"
"Fran has the final forms I need to sign. I'll need to connect my pen tablet to sign them and I'm short a port. I need to do this now, okay?"
"Fine. I'll go for a walk. Maybe I'll see an aurora."
"If you do, come get me."

...

Light was fading, but annoyingly, the place had as many light poles as the cities where they'd stayed and it was going to be another night without stars. Why did all the northern Canada towns have so many street lights? He had better luck seeing the night sky in California and he would never have expected that.

The motel rooms were obviously portable buildings that had been trucked in. They were nice, and their room had a new look. Considering how vacant the road had been, there were enough rooms for local workers as well.

He found the cylinder in the cab of the pickup and checked the reading. 42.91. His heart sank.

So, the magic spot isn't on this stretch of road. The bearing number was climbing, from that minimum of just under 30 down at the St. Lawrence. Now it was pointing more and more eastward, and according to the map, the point where they reached Labrador was to the north.

It was discouraging. Biz would make them turn around and they were still no closer to discovering the source of the cylinder. He'd make that argument, but it was getting old. She was ready to go back home.

There were a couple of other cars here. So they weren't the only people on the road, but if this was the only place to stay in hundreds of miles... kilometers, then these other two vehicles must be the bulk of the travelers on Labrador Highway.

He stashed the GPS back in the truck, and was a little startled to see a man resting against another pickup just a few units down, smoking. He nodded. "Hi. I see your tags. Are you from California?"

"Yes. Fresno, actually."

"What brings you up this way?"

"Oh, just a vacation trip. Seeing what we can see. Where are you from?"

"Churchill Falls, in Labrador. The wife and I went down to Montréal on holiday."

Another man came out onto the porch of his unit. "Is that English I hear?"

The newcomer was retired, from Wisconsin. He and his wife had been several days in Québec and they were having the same feelings of isolation as Seth.

The Labrador man, being the local expert, was quickly quizzed about the road up ahead.

"It's dirt, almost all the way to Goose Bay. But there's a little rain, and that'll help keep the dust down."

When the Wisconsin man found out that they had Internet, he begged the chance to get online and make their ferry reservations out of Goose Bay. They were heading on to Newfoundland. Seth was glad to offer the help. The man called to his wife and told her the news.

Biz answered the door. When she saw strangers with Seth, she fumbled out, "Bonjour?"

"Oh, no. English, English!"

She was almost done with her uploads of the signed papers and was happy to invite the older lady in. With travel brochures in hand, and the web page to look up, they got to business.

With someone to talk to, Biz brightened up. She looked happier than he'd seen her in days. Seth went back outside where the men were talking about the roads and what to expect up ahead. He was the man of their expedition, so he wanted to hear that as well.

The man from Churchill Falls was a character. Seth had missed his name the first time and he was too timid to ask again.

"Oh, the road isn't *too* bad. See my truck with the raised suspension and the 8-ply tires?"

The white-haired man from Wisconsin looked pale as he considered his own loaded down camper pickup.

The machinist chuckled and waved. "Just kidding. You won't have any trouble with the highway."

When he had enough of the chill, and the conversation was winding down for the evening, Seth went back in. The ladies were still chatting away about what things to go see if they went on to Newfoundland.

He was surprised to hear Biz asking about the ferries at Goose Bay. Had she changed her mind? Was she really considering going on all the way to the Atlantic?

As the Wisconsin lady left, she gave Biz a stack of maps–duplicates of one's she'd ordered before her trip. She'd done her research and been prepared.

"Did you see anything in the sky?"

Seth shook his head. "I didn't even see the stars. I couldn't tell if it was clouds or just glare from the street lights."

"Well, all the paperwork is done. Fran will deposit the check into our account. We have our safety net."

She held out the Newfoundland map. "Do you think we should go on this far?"

It was more than he'd expected. "Ask me when we find the magic spot."

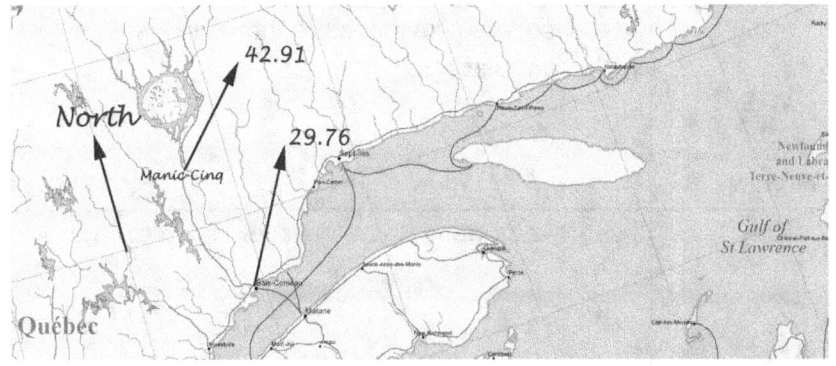

Chapter 8: Driving Dirt

They were the last tourists to leave the Manic-Cinq island of civilization. Once again, a soft bed made it hard to get up in the morning. Again, he had no expectation of network connection for several hundred kilometers, so he begged Biz to delay shutting down her connection for a few minutes.

...

nickyWhy	@SethPartner Hey, I tried to look up Labrador. Seems Labrador and Newfoundland are one province. I thought they were two different things.
SaraCMe	@nickyWhy Well, duh! Everybody knows that.
moosenine	@SaraCMe I thought @SethPartner was in Canada.

ClaraN1	@moosenine provinces are things like states. Only canadian.
SethPartner	I see everyone is up before me. How was the game?
moosenine	@SethPartner Nick couldn't shut up. Yack, yack, yack. I'd like to meet him on the field.
nickyWhy	@moosenine You'd have to catch me first.

...

Once on the road, Seth looked at the cylinder again.

"Probably today," Biz nodded. "At the rate we're going, if we push it, we should cross the bearing heading east, once we reach Labrador."

"Did you know Labrador and Newfoundland are one province?"

She frowned, "No. I always thought they were two."

"And they speak English." He wanted to remind her of that.

Not too far north from the Manic-Cinq road stop, they saw the dam, with a tall string of arches crossing the valley. He unfolded their new Québec Province map.

"Lake Manicouagan. Looks weird. Circular."

"It's a giant meteor crater," she said. "I read the tourist info last night.

A three mile wide asteroid hit here 214 million years ago. The road goes through the mountains around its edge."

"Cool. I wish I'd known that this morning."

"To tell the gang?" She grinned.

"Hey, I don't think Moose has ever once left Fresno. Probably won't, unless he gets a football scholarship. They ask what I'm doing."

She shrugged. "Maybe if Manic-Cinq had Internet, maybe the place we stop next will too."

...

It was indeed a dirt road as they left the dam area. But his guide from Labrador was right. It was a good dirt road, wide and smooth. And there was a faint misting in the air, which reduced the dust somewhat.

As they crossed the crest of a mountain ridge, the road got very steep, much steeper than anything they were used to in the USA. "It's a 20% grade, I bet." Biz shifted the pickup down to keep from using the brakes. This was not the kind of place to burn out your brake pads.

"Look, that's the people from Wisconsin." He recognized the tiny white pickup camper far ahead in the distance. If it weren't for their dust plume, he might have missed them altogether. As they went down the slope, they were again hidden by the next hill.

"This is part of a meteor crater, right?"

"That's what I read."

Seth looked around. The lake with its large central island just looked like a regular reservoir anywhere. "I guess it's too big to see its shape. Only map makers and astronauts could notice it."

She nodded. "Too close to see anything but the nearest mile. 'Can't see the forest for the trees'."

He smiled. The trees here were very narrow and dark green, with not much in the way of side branches. The dark made quite a contrast with the lush green of the brushy growth next to the road. There was a wider swath that had been cleared some years back. It was pretty and definitely wild, but this was nothing like the redwoods back on the coast. The further north they went, the smaller the trees got.

...

"Stop here."

Biz pulled over, although since there was no traffic, she could have just stopped in the middle of the highway with no risk.

"I want to take a picture of this." He pointed to the ground, thickly covered with splotchy green lichens. There were several kinds, light green, dark green, gray, and white. Tiny little trees, no more than a couple of feet tall were scattered through the area.

Biz had gotten out as he took his pictures, and stretched.

"Is this tundra?" he asked.

She shrugged. "Maybe. It sorta matches what I've heard. I guess that's not too surprising, is it?"

"Do you want me to drive?"

"Fine."

...

Driving dirt took a little practice. It was too easy to go faster than you could control. That wasn't pavement under the tires. Gravel could roll if he touched the brakes. Don't go fast, and be ready to slow down gradually. He got the hang of it, but by the time the glimpses of the lake were more in the rear view mirror than to the side, he was constantly having to remind himself to slow down.

Then came the bridge. A wide torrent of greenish water crossed from somewhere off to the northeast, presumably moving toward Lake Manicouagan. For a dirt road, he guessed he shouldn't have been surprised at a wooden bridge. It was hefty and well-built, but it was definitely a one-lane bridge with boards laid out where his tires were supposed to go. Biz didn't comment when he slowed to a crawl as he passed over.

"This is a highway?"

She nodded. "Yep. Biggest road in this part of the province."

...

Barely five miles later, the rumble of the road changed. "Hey! Pavement." He sped up.

A minute later, "Uh, Biz." She was dozing.

"Yeah?"

"There are sidewalks here."

"What?"

They slowed down and tried to make sense of what they were seeing.

The road was paved. It had curbs, and there were cross streets to nothing but empty ground, with sidewalks along the highway.

"It's like there used to be a town here."

"Yeah, but not like a ghost town. They must have taken everything when they left. There're no buildings. No ruins. No nothing. Just the road."

As they crept along at five miles per hour, looking at what had been the site of some kind of settlement, the curbs and sidewalks dropped away. But there was still pavement. He sped back up.

Biz looked at her maps. "This one has a spot marked Gagnon. I guess there was a town here once. I'm glad we filled up our tanks back at Manic-Cinq rather than hope for a gas station here."

He nodded. "Don't trust the maps."

...

The pavement lasted until they reached a sign that proclaimed Site Minier De Fire Lake. There was evidence of long abandoned mine tailings. When the road reverted to gravel he asked, "Do you think the missing town and the abandoned mine were related? Is that the reason for the paved stretch of road?"

Biz shrugged. "I have a lot of questions, once I get back to civilization."

She dug out the cylinder and checked the readings again. "The bearing keeps increasing. We'll need to head east before too long."

He had nothing to say about that. They were on the road. The only road as far as he knew. If the mystery spot was off in the wilds, they'd never find it.

...

"The Wisconsin folks." Their white camper was parked next to a pond and the couple were staring out at the water. Seth pulled to a stop as they waved.

"Loons," the man pointed, holding his binoculars. They watched a group of four of the birds in the water, giving an alert cry, disturbed by people in their area. It was the bird on the dollar coin.

"They're very territorial," the white-haired man explained. "Usually you only see a single pair in a pond like this. Two of those are probably this year's young ones. A family unit."

Seth looked closer through the offered binoculars. Which one was the Seth and which one was the Biz?

When the birds moved farther away from shore, their calls became less strident and more haunting.

As Seth drove off, he said, "It's good we got a chance to pass them. With all the road dust, I'd hate to be following them for mile after mile."

...

The next mine they saw, less than an hour later, was very much alive. He'd been expecting something, because in addition to the tiny tree forest, there were now more signs of civilization; railroad tracks, portable buildings, cross roads and even occasional traffic. But the mine was obviously the center of it all. Huge trucks, earth movers, were taking apart one mountain and building another with the dregs. If there was a sign that named or explained what was being dug up, he didn't see it. It was probably all in French anyway.

Then, there was a road intersection; the turnoff to Fermont.

"Do we go there, or move on to Labrador City?"

Biz chewed her lip. "Don't pass up the chance for a gas station, and a bathroom." So they turned right. As she dashed inside at the gas station, he looked over at the dormitory building. He wouldn't have been surprised to see something like that at a big city university. Four stories tall, and several blocks long, with a spacious parking lot, it had to be the residence for the people working the mine. There were only windows on the top three floors. A snow issue? If there were regular houses anywhere, they weren't where he could see them. Fermont was a company town, no doubt about it.

Biz took over the driving, and just a few more miles, back on the main highway, there was a large blue sign, saying "Newfoundland Labrador" and "Welcome to the Big Land".

"I told you Newfoundland and Labrador were one province."

She didn't bother to reply.

After the small dormitory town of Fermont, Labrador City looked huge. It was a city, with houses, and paved streets and....

"Biz, do you see that!"

"What?"

"There's a Walmart here!"

"No, really?"

After so many miles on the road into the north, a city was indeed a marvel.

"Check our bearing, and pull out the map." She found a shoulder near an intersection.

The cylinder reported 70.51.

"Wow. We have to go east. Is this the intersection?"

The map showed Highway 500, the Trans Labrador Highway, the biggest highway in Labrador, and it was the only highway heading east towards the Atlantic. And it was another dirt road.

Chapter 9: Churchill Falls

A hundred kilometers eastward from Labrador City, they stopped by a water crossing to make sandwiches. Seth got out to take a better look at the road.

The highway was still dirt, but it was the best engineered dirt road he'd ever seen. The landscape, for miles upon miles was flat, swampy terrain, with a few of the small dark trees here and there. From time to time, he saw stretches of the original highway off in the distance. It was just a simple path more suited to a Jeep or a motorcycle, moving up and down and side to side and across numerous creeks. Taking that trail would have slowed them down to a crawl.

But this road, the new one, was raised about eight feet above the landscape. It was straight as a landing strip for miles at a time and it was wide enough for passing lanes and pull offs, if it were just paved. Several times they had seen places where hillsides had been pulverized for the road base to make this raised platform. In fact, the bulk of the traffic on this road were the work crews themselves.

Biz was checking the map and watching the readout on the cylinder. "I wish we had a real traveler's GPS. I don't think the route on the map matches this road."

"Any sign that we're getting near the magic spot?"

"Not really. I can tell we're getting closer, however. The readings get more erratic by the hour."

"But we're still headed the right direction?"

"Yes, but we really don't have a choice. It's this way or head back home."

He nodded. This was a lonely place. Off to the left, standing water in a boggy field looked like it would trap anyone who tried to hike through this land. Maybe moose liked it.

Come winter, it'd all be frozen solid. That might be the best time to explore Labrador. A snowmobile would be right at home in this flat land. Of course, you'd have to haul your own fuel. Maybe dog sleds would be better.

Back near Labrador City, he'd seen portable sheds that had been left out near ponds. He'd thought maybe they were fishing sheds, but the best way to move something like that would be towing it with a snowmobile. Any wheeled vehicle would be stuck in the mud. When everything was frozen, you could just drag your shed to the edge of your favorite fishing pond and leave it there until the spring thaw.

"I'd hate to have a garden here."

Seth had to agree. "You'd need a greenhouse." It occurred to him that he hadn't seen any. "No crops. No farms. No livestock. I guess they have to import all their food."

Except maybe fish and moose. What else? Caribou. Are there deer this far north? He just didn't know.

"There are local tribes, I'm sure. But I bet they live on the coast."

"I don't know. People seem to live everywhere."

"Yeah. Even Fresno."

She chuckled. "Without the highways and the railroads and the hundred some water wells, it'd be a pretty tough place to live. I've heard Fresno's ten inches of rain per year is right at the technical definition of a desert."

"Hmm. Do you think Aunt Ally is watering your flowers?"

She sighed. "I'm not going to think about that."

"Sorry I brought it up."

...

Seth slowed down when the dust got too thick. "I'm not going to try to pass those guys on motorcycles. The visibility is so bad I wouldn't be able to see if someone was coming the other direction."

"Fine by me. Let them get farther ahead. I don't want to breathe this stuff all the way across Labrador either."

She checked the bearing again and sighed.

"Anything?"

"No. Still up ahead. I guess."

"Problem?"

"No, I just worry that this number is due to some stuck memory cell, and not the real source of the cylinder. I'd really hate to have come thousands of miles, all the way across the continent, and have it turn out to be just a fluke."

He slowed even more as they passed over a flowing stream. There was something, like a wire cage, in the water. Someone's fish trap, or maybe it was for a water mammal. He couldn't tell.

"I don't mind. This has been a great trip, and I'll have lots of stories to tell, once I get back on the net. If we'd have gone straight home, you'd be yelling at me to get off the computer and feeling sorry for yourself about your job."

"You don't think I was just over-reacting to Jess and acting silly?"

"Of course I do, but it's okay. I wanted to solve our little mystery too. More than you did. I'm grateful for Jess acting like a jerk. I don't think we'd ever have stayed on the road this long without a little help."

...

Biz was driving when they reached the bridge over the Churchill River. She pulled to a stop right in the middle.

A huge waterfall must have been coursing below, in the past. Now it was a extensive, rocky channel, long ago scoured clean of anything but massive boulders. A small trickle of water traced the route where torrents must have passed.

"I know what this is."

"Churchill Falls," she said.

"Yeah, but it's missing the water. Just like Great Falls and all those other places we saw. There has to be a hydroelectric power plant near here."

"Check the cylinder."

He pulled it out. "113.58, but the lower digit keeps flickering."

"Closer and closer."

"There's a town named Churchill Falls. It has to be nearby."

"There'd better be. It's time to fill the gas tank again."

"That guy I met at Manic-Cinq said he was from there. I bet he works for the power plant."

She drove on. There were roads branching off, and soon, they saw a landing strip.

"Got its own airport."

"What's the reading?"

"137.59"

She pointed off to the right side of the road. "Our mystery spot has to be in that direction."

Soon, there were signs for local businesses. "The gas station is that way." She turned and drove into the little town.

At first glance, Churchill Falls looked like any small town. There were houses and kids playing in a school yard. The gas station was a two-pump stop with a little store. A kid a little younger than Seth stepped out to come pump the gas.

"The cylinder says 275.59."

"Wow. We passed it. It might be in the town."

It was exciting, now that they were so close. He set the cylinder down on the floor and got out to talk to the kid. Biz hurriedly dashed for the store. Long distances between towns were harder on her than on him. He didn't mind stopping by the side of the road to relieve bladder pressure, but she didn't care to do that.

The kid was ready to pump the gas. Seth was used to it by now. The idea that everyone had to pump their own gas had been left behind in California.

"Is there any military base near here?"

He shrugged. "No, nothing like that. We get travelers, hunters and fishermen. Tourists in the summer. Where are you from?"

"California. Just traveling. What's interesting near here?"

He chuckled. "Nothing. 200 kilometers that way to Labrador City and 300 kilometers the other way to Goose Bay, with nothing in between. But we've got good fishing. And there's a tour of the power plant."

"Is there Internet anywhere?"

"Sure, at Town Centre."

Seth took his cell phone out of his pocket. The screen flickered. The battery was dead. He reached into the truck and put it back on the charger.

Pickup filled, he followed the local kid into the shop. Biz was chatting with the lady behind the counter.

"I've got us a place to stay for the night. But the fancy place is all booked up. Our place has no Internet."

They paid for the gas and Biz drove through the little town. "It's still someplace west of here." He set the cylinder down.

"I bet that's Town Centre." It was the largest building around, three stories tall in places. Just glancing at it from the outside, it appeared to be both the school, the motel that had been filled up before they arrived, and probably more. It looked like a place that had been built in sections, rather than the uniform dormitory style place they'd seen back in Fermont.

The houses that made up the bulk of the town seemed standardized, like two story modular homes that had been built in some factory. Some were different colors, and everyone's cars and trucks were different, but it looked nothing like the houses he'd grown up with. He wondered if it were the result of living up here in the north. There were trees, but nothing big enough to support any logging industry. If everything had to be shipped in hundreds of kilometers over dirt roads, did that mean these houses came that way too?

The whole town was a puzzle. But it wasn't the mystery spot. They had yet to find it. But if it were close, it wasn't likely a military base like he'd half expected.

"We have lots of daylight left, let's retrace the road."

Biz drove slowly, and he called out the GPS readings as they headed back toward the landing strip. When it read 180.00, she stopped. "It's due south from here. Maybe on the other side of this hill. But there's no road to get there."

"How far away is it, do you think?"

"Maybe a mile. I don't know. We'd have to walk it, and cross that creek."

The water was close to the road and Seth didn't relish mucking his way through it. "Not this evening."

"No. We'll have more time to look around tomorrow. Let's go find this Black Spruce Lodge."

"Black spruce. Is that the little trees that we've been seeing?"

"Probably."

She had a set of directions, so they went back to the gas station and found John Cabot Street and the lodge. There were no lighted motel signs, or vacancy signs, but it was the right address. Seth got out of the pickup and hesitantly stuck his head in.

No one was there, but there was a sign to take off your shoes. He did, and they found their room number.

The lodge wasn't a motel like he'd imagined. There was a common kitchen, dining room, and laundry. Their room had a couple of beds, but that was it.

"I'm going to take advantage of the laundry while we have it."

"Supposedly the Town Centre has Internet. I'd like to take my phone and see if I can pick up some Wi-Fi."

She drove him back in the pickup. He was glad for the opportunity to continue charging his phone. "If I can't find anything, I'll just walk back. It's not far."

Inside, he saw that the Town Centre was a little bit of everything. There was the library, the school, a restaurant, the bank, the motel that had no rooms for them, a grocery store, various administration type places, a sports center, and the 'Curling Club', whatever that was.

Risking the Wrath of Biz, he turned his cell phone back on and looked for signal. He'd seen a cell tower in the town, but it must have been on a different band or system, because his phone showed no signal at all. He deactivated the cell phone part and checked for Wi-Fi.

Bars!

...

| moosenine | I know what curling is. They had a thing on espn. They take a tea pot and slide it down the ice and shake brooms at it. |

SethPartner	@moosenine Seriously?
moosenine	seriously, it was big time last winter olympics.
SaraCme	I see you found Internet. Where are you?
SethPartner	@SaraCMe Sitting in the lobby of this Town Center place. Churchill Falls is the town. Probably the only town around here.

The icon for a private message popped up. He switched modes.

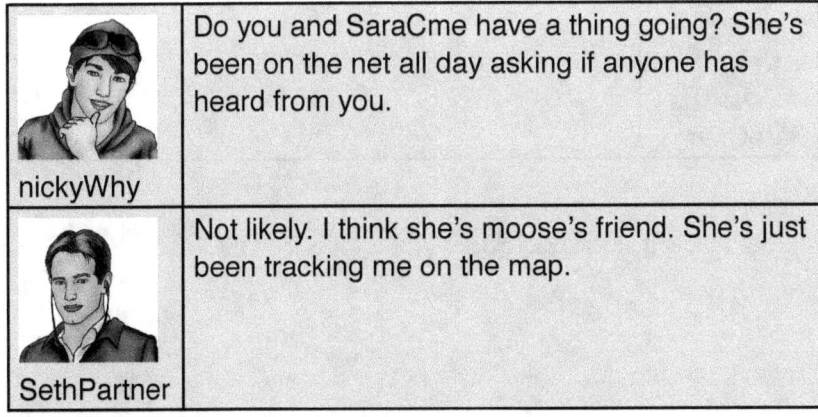

nickyWhy	Do you and SaraCme have a thing going? She's been on the net all day asking if anyone has heard from you.
SethPartner	Not likely. I think she's moose's friend. She's just been tracking me on the map.

He switched back to public messages.

moosenine	they prbly got hockey. All those snowy places have hockey. Did you ever see Mystery Alaska? Excellent movie.
nickyWhy	If, as you say, the mystery spot is near you, then you'd better watch your step. Your cylinder went xthousand miles. Someone's protecting it
moosenine	Yeah, watcher back for Canadian secret agents. They act all wishy-washy, but ya seen all the kick-ass tv shows that come out of Canada?
nickyWhy	And what's with this town in the middle of nowhere. That's suspicious. Maybe it's a secret science base like Eureka.
SaraCMe	@SethPartner What time zone are you in?

Seth looked at the wall clock.

SethPartner	@SaraCMe It's 11:20
nickyWhy	@SethPartner That's like 4 time zones. You're farther east than NYC I guess.
SethPartner	Well, it's getting late here. I didn't notice cause the sunset time is later this far north. Biz will be worrying. l8tr

And his cell phone was running warm. He'd need to charge it again soon. But it had been nice to get back in touch with the gang and update them on all that he'd seen. Travel was cool, but he needed a satellite network link or something if he were going to be spending all this time so far from civilization.

...

Stepping outside, he looked at the sleepy little town lit by street lights. There were hardly any cars, but there were a number of people out walking or on bicycles.

But...which way was his room? It looked different and he hadn't actually paid much attention to landmarks when Biz dropped him off. When all the houses in the town look nearly identical, he needed better navigation cues.

He walked towards the corner, hoping to see a street sign. It was Cabot street, or something like that.

A red haired girl about his age came out of the Town Centre behind him. Pretty.

"Excuse me? Do you know which direction the Black Spruce Lodge is?"
She smiled and laughed. "Yes, Seth. I do. Just follow me."

...

He stood there for a few heartbeats, with his mouth open. "How...what did you say?"

"It's me, Sarah. Sarah Clarke. SaraCMe. I've been waiting for you to get here for days now."

He didn't know how to react. In his mind, SaraCMe was in California. Barstow California. She couldn't have teleported here.

She laughed again. "Close your mouth and follow me." She turned and walked away. He followed.

They'd barely gone half a block when the crunchy sound of another set of shoes on gravel made him turn his head. The kid from the gas station trotted up.

"Hi. I see you've met my sister."

In the distance, two more teens were coming to join them. Seth hurried to catch up with Sarah.

"You've been following me?"

She nodded. "Yes, since you first typed the marking number of the cylinder into twitter. I was googling for it and your tweets showed up. Search engines are wonderful."

One of the new guys asked, "What about the sister?"

Sarah said, "Terry is already there."

Chapter 10: Stranger Friends

The troop of them, the four locals leading the way, walked through the darkened, orange tinted town and Seth struggled to make sense of it.

SaraCMe is a spy! He looked at her closely, but she looked just like any girl he'd have met at school. Nick's worry about Canadian spies just didn't seem to match up with these kids. *I thought she was one of Moose's girl friends.* The football hero of the Fresno Warriors often showed up with a new tag-along girl friend. *She claimed to be from Barstow.* He struggled to remember everything he knew about her from her tweets. There was something about her not being able to find a game at the store. It certainly made more sense here than in Barstow.

And she had seemed interested in my travel stops. It had been flattering. But she was just interested in getting the cylinder. That was plain. The big question was whether Biz and he were in any danger.

The impulse to make a mad sprint for the Black Spruce Lodge was cut short by the knowledge that his entourage knew the location better than he did and that there was already someone there who had his sister.

The cell phone in his pocket was useless. He couldn't even send an alert out to the gang. If they vanished, here in this strange town at the edge of the known universe, as far as people with cars are concerned, would they even know to contact someone?

Tomorrow, when the gang asked about him, Sarah could claim a private message from him saying they had moved on towards Goose Bay and no one would have the slightest clue about what happened.

Who could help? Were these people on the side of the Canadian government or not? Would calling in the police just be sidetracked by some dark secret organization?

Seth tried to calm down. He was starting to worry like Nick did when he got caught up in some Internet conspiracy theory. Nobody had tried to hurt him. They weren't even watching to make sure he didn't try to bolt. Not that there was any place to go.

He saw his silver gray pickup as they turned a corner, and parked next to it was a darker pickup. He couldn't tell its color in this light. As they entered, everyone kicked off their shoes.

Biz was sitting at the common table, chatting brightly with a man about her age.

"Oh, there you are. I was wondering if I were going to have to go chase you down. Seth, this is...."

"Terry."

She looked puzzled. "Yes. Terry Kelly. And who are your friends?"

"Biz, we found them. Or rather, they found us. These are the cylinder people."

Biz looked at Terry, a with a bit of alarm. He nodded, embarrassed. "Yes, we knew you were coming. Sarah has been monitoring Seth's tweets ever since you found our package."

Biz frowned. "Who are you?"

Terry shrugged, "It's nothing sinister. We're just something like a model rocket club. We launched an instrumented package and we were surprised it got as far as California."

He looked embarrassed. "We were expecting fifty or a hundred kilometers at best. When we lost radio contact in the launch phase, we thought it was gone forever. It was supposed to radio back its GPS location, so we could go find it either now, or when the snows made snowmobile trips possible. We half expected to lose it in the lakes, or in the swamps, but it was Sarah's job to search the Internet and when she found your references so quickly, we debated contacting you up front.

"I suppose we should have just contacted Seth's email address and made arrangements to have it shipped to us, but we took so long debating the issue that you were heading our way before we made any decision. So, Sarah followed your group of friends and when you started getting close, we had Kolton here keep an eye out for your pickup. We knew you had to stop there for gas and he was ready with good excuses if you were planning to head on to Goose Bay immediately."

Biz seemed somewhat relieved. "Well, I think you should have been up front about it and contacted us, but your cylinder is right out in the truck. Seth, would you go get it?"

Sarah and Kolton followed him out. He handed it to the kid.

"What a mess!"

Back at the table. Terry put on a pair of glasses and frowned at the mangled end.

"Wow, it must have hit hard. You can hardly see the camera." He had a tool kit with him and carefully pried open the mangled portion where the shell had smashed in.

Biz commented, "I didn't even see that seam, and I looked it over pretty carefully."

"There's a small digital camera. See here. But the impact has shattered it to bits. Even the memory card is damaged." He cautiously poked at the fragments through a large illuminated magnifying glass that had its own tripod. "I may be able to salvage the chip."

Biz nodded. "I certainly can. This is my field. Do you have another card that I can scavenge the leads from."

He handed the magnifying glass and tools over to her and she set to work.

It was plain that Biz and Terry were completely absorbed in the delicate electronic task. Seth looked at the others.

"A model rocket club, huh? Do you have any other rockets? We had a club like that in Fresno. I helped with a rocket that used an M-class engine just last year, but you must have launched a monster to get to California. Do you have any pictures?" The hesitancy and the looks between the group said much. Sarah said, "We'll show you later."

He felt the need to push, to see what he could find out. Addressing the guys, "Well, in case you don't know, I'm Seth Palmer. That's my sister Biz...Elizabeth."

A hand came out, "I'm Don Hamby. This is Bill Heath. I guess you've already met KC and Sarah."

He shook hands. "So you're all part of this model rocket club?"

"It's Terry's club. Just a sort of school science club. He's the sponsor."

Bill looked uncomfortable and glanced at his watch. "I've got to get on home."

"Um. Me too." Don nodded. "I guess we'll talk later." They went to recover their shoes and escape.

Sarah said, "KC, go on home, too. If Dad asks, tell him I'm on my way. I'm at a late game at the Teen Centre."

He nodded and left.

Biz was deep in the electronics, and probably didn't even notice the people leaving. As she'd said, this kind of stuff was her field. Seth didn't begrudge her the opportunity to play. Besides, if there was a camera, and it had managed to save images on that memory card, then he'd like to see what was there.

He'd launched a couple of model rockets of his own, and joined in with groups launching larger ones. Some of those had carried cameras. That and a life long interest in the space program kept him from feeling too panicked about being led into this trap. He would have put up with a lot more to get into some kind of real space program. No matter what they were hiding, it seemed that they had succeeded in launching a probe that had gone thousands of miles. That was much more than any model rocket he knew about.

Sarah was looking at him. He moved to the sitting room and she followed. The chairs were old and well used. But they were comfortable enough.

"So, how much of what you said on Twitter was the truth?"

She shrugged, looking down at her hands. "I didn't talk much about myself. The profile said I lived in Barstow. I just plucked that town off a map and made sure I didn't say anything specific. It was just for window dressing."

"I thought you were Moose's girlfriend."

"I didn't say that. When I located your tweet with the code number, I just chose one of your friends to follow first and then added the rest as I was 'introduced'."

"Sneaky."

"Moose does sound cute, in a muscular sort of way."

"Don't tell him you ran a scam on him. Be sure and let him down gently. We kidded him about you, and you didn't deny it. He gets his feelings hurt, even though you'd never know it from his tweets."

She frowned a little. "I never wanted to hurt anyone. I just needed a way to track you and following all your friends meant I wouldn't miss out on parts of the conversation."

"Other than DMs–direct messages."

"What?"

"DMs are private. One to one tweets that no one else can see. You didn't see what Nick said about you this evening, did you?"

"No. What?"

He shook his head. It was mean, he knew, but she had started the deception.

She protested. "Twitter is public, you know that!"

"Yeah, it's all our fault for expecting people to be honest. You know you ran a scam on us. On me. You wanted to track me, so you sent the right lies to get that information."

"I don't want to talk about this."

"Okay." *Just don't expect me to trust anything you say, ever again.*

She looked over at the table where Biz and Terry were working. They were crouched over the wires and the only thing he could hear through the open doorway from his position was Biz when she laughed. Whatever Terry was selling, she was buying.

He wished there was Wi-Fi signal here. Yes, Nick was paranoid from too many games and Moose would want to knock heads and Clara would probably think he was just crazy, but he wished he could at least talk about it. This town...Labrador...all of Canada even–it was isolated. At least it was for him with his fancy cell phone designed for service down south in the USA. He'd likely have a better chance of contacting them over a land-line, with voice. That is if he had his friends' phone numbers written down somewhere.

...

"Tell me about your rocket. It must have been huge to reach California. The biggest one I've ever seen used a single M engine. What size did you use?"

Her eyes widened a little as she stumbled. "Yes. It was a...big engine. Terry knows all that stuff."

She stood up. "Terry?"

He didn't really look up from peering through the magnifying glass. He had a soldering iron in hand and there was a faint trace of smoke rising from the wires. Even the air smelled faintly of hot resin.

"Yes, Sarah?"

"I need to go home now."

"Okay, I'll see you tomorrow then."

She turned to Seth and started to say something but shook her head and went to collect her shoes.

He moved to her chair, which had a better view of his sister, and settled in to wait. Maybe they had no need to keep him under watch day and night, but he wasn't about to let Biz out of his sight. There was still too much he didn't know about these people. Were they criminals of some kind? Could it be just something innocent like firing rockets without a license? Or was Nick right after all, and they were some kind of Canadian secret organization that just happened to use kids?

One thing was becoming clear. If they shot rockets, it wasn't using the standardized engine categories everyone else used. Sarah had been totally clueless when he mentioned the class M engine, and everyone in model rocketry knew about the standard engine sizes. Your first model likely used one of the little A engines, and by the time you were wanting more power than the D-class motors you could buy at the hobby shops, you discovered the organized clubs and the bigger engines that kept climbing up right through the alphabet.

No matter what they were keeping secret, she had lied and tricked him. Being pretty didn't make her trustworthy. He'd have to be careful and watch everthing she did.

Chapter 11: Pictures Tell the Story

Terry's chair scooting back from the table, wood on wood, brought Seth back from a doze.

"That's the best I can test without hooking it up to my laptop. I've got an memory card reader we can disassemble. Are you up for it? It's getting late."

Biz nodded. "I'm used to all-nighters. Let's see this through." He left, with the maze of wires and clamps and tools in the middle of the table.

As soon as he heard the engine start outside, Seth asked, "Who are these people? I'm really worried we may be mixed up in something criminal. We might be a security risk to them."

She laughed, "Hardly that! Terry's science club is nothing more than a group like that one at Hobbytown. How often did you bug me for money to buy another rocket engine or a set of igniters?"

"Biz, those rockets I shot could travel a thousand feet, with a good wind. The biggest shot I saw at that Tripoli event had an M-class engine and went up 11,000 feet and came down a mile or so from the launch site.

"That was a big engine. No way is there a model rocket club that is launching something that comes down *on the other side if the continent!*

"And Sarah didn't even know what I was talking about when I mentioned an M-class engine. That kinda stuff is what rocket guys talk about all the time! It's like you talking with your computer friends and never mentioning CPU type or clock speed or stuff like that.

"Terry's club is not a model rocket club. I don't know what it is."

She didn't see the problem.

"Terry isn't going to do anything to us. This is just a school sponsored science club. Now Terry is really smart, his instrument probe is first rate. Maybe they've just discovered a better rocket engine than you're familiar with.

"In any case, they aren't going to kidnap us or anything like that. For one thing, your twitter friends all know where you are, don't they?"

"But why didn't they contact us when they realized we had the cylinder? Why trick us? That sounds criminal to me!"

...

They were still arguing when Terry came back with a big smile and a computer bag. Biz didn't even bother to bring up her brother's worries.

"Let me see the card reader." He was again ignored, and he went out to the pickup to get something with caffeine to drink.

The town was silent. It certainly looked like a nice peaceful place. If it weren't for the ever present street lights and the uniform appearance of the houses, it could have been any small town back in California.

He found a place to sit next to the pickup where most of the street lights were obscured by the lodge or the vehicles and stared up at the few stars dotting the glow saturated sky.

What if Terry's club had managed to discover a new kind of engine? The evidence insisted that their cylinder had been up beyond the atmosphere, unless it was even a bigger lie and they had built a drone aircraft or something like that. What was that phrase? Getting above the atmosphere was half-way to anywhere. Something like that. If Terry had strapped a hefty rocket engine to the cylinder and had given it a second-stage boost, he might have put the thing into orbit.

What a concept! A high school science club joining the space-faring nations.

Would I have tricked someone like Sarah did if I were on the inside of that group?

They were still at it when he came back inside and settled into the chair to watch.

Biz and Terry hacked apart the memory card reader and had it mated with the mess on the table soon enough. Cautiously, Terry connected the USB cable and his software began copying the image files onto his laptop.

When the thousands of files were pulled in, he clicked on the first and saw a picture of a blurry hand.

Seth stood up and moved to where he could see the screen.

"I had started the camera and we were sealing up the probe." He started a slideshow of the whole set of photos. At first, there were just cables, like a wire fence and Kolton Clarke walking around on the outside of it. It was night time, and everything was lit by a bank of utility lights.

"The camera was aimed out the side."

Then, the fence dropped away and the camera auto-exposure brought up details in the darkness. It was climbing rapidly above the landscape, showing the lake and ponds lit by moonlight. And then there was more.

"Oh," said Biz. "Is that an aurora?"

"Yes, it was bright that night."

Auroral glow filled the frame as the land dropped entirely away. There were a few bright stars beyond, but the glow shifted from frame to frame, getting closer by the second. And then something must have happened to the probe, because there were streaks across the sky, like a meteor shower, and the image was tumbling.

"I guess that's when the parachute system ripped away. There's no sign of it. You didn't see any plastic case around the cylinder when you found it did you?"

Seth shook his head. "No. Just what we brought back."

Terry clicked through the slide show manually because it was all becoming a blur.

"We lost it somehow." He started fast scanning through the rest of the images, but other than an occasional streak of light, there was nothing. "So much for a clear image of its path. I've got to hope that the tracking info in the GPS has survived. But that's a job for tomorrow."

Biz said, "It's amazing that you got it to work at all. Seth has been telling me how much better your launch was than the model rockets he's used to seeing back in California. And your instrument package! I knew it was first rate work back when we first opened it up. And then, I didn't even know about the camera."

Seth didn't interrupt. He watched Terry nod and say nothing. There was a lot he wasn't talking about.

And there was a lot Seth noticed about the images.

A camera movie from a rocket launch was almost standard on the big launches. He'd seen dozens.

They were all shot in daylight. Why had Terry's club launched at night?

There hadn't been a hint of rocket glare or smoke, and with that side view, the landscape should have been well lit by it in the first seconds of the flight. Nor was there any hint it was any kind of drone aircraft. It was going straight up.

From what he could tell, as the image shifted, the rocket was still accelerating rapidly long after a rocket engine would have shut down.

And it went above the aurora lights. Just how high did it go?

...

Terry packed up his tool kit and laptop. Biz walked him out to his car. The lodge seemed very quiet. Were they the only ones in the place? The hotel over at Town Centre was supposedly fully booked. The check-in for the Black Spruce was there at the gas station. Could Terry's club have misrepresented the other place? Had Biz actually called around? KC, Sarah's brother, worked there. Anything was possible.

It would have been so much better to be in a public place, with Internet, rather than isolated over here in this deserted lodge.

The cylinder, with its attached wiring was still taking up the dining room table. If there had been other customers, they couldn't have left it sitting out there in the open like that.

Biz came back inside. The whimsical smile on her face turned serious when she saw him. "You're still worried about him, aren't you?"

"Somebody has to. Do you mean to say that you have no worries about his story?"

"No. And you shouldn't either. I trust him, so butt out. Rule Six, remember."

"Don't forget Rule Four. I haven't."

"Seth, don't worry about it. We're in no danger. Now, I've got a load of laundry to get dry before tomorrow and I'm looking forward to a nice long bath. It's very late, so I need to get started."

Arguing was useless. She was convinced he was only worried about her interest in Terry as a guy. She didn't see the other issues. He resisted the urge to continue. He was serious about Rule Four, however; *I'll take care of you and you'll take care of me.*

Unfortunately, in the absence of a smoking gun, the Rule Six prohibition about sniping at each other's romantic interests overruled Rule Four's general concern. He'd need better evidence to convince her, or even make her listen.

When she headed for the bathroom, towels and bathrobe in hand, he went into their bedroom and pulled her laptop out of the travel case.

Biz had set up an independent account on her laptop for him to use on the trip, since his computer back at home was a clunky desktop tower better designed to run games than for portability. Six months ago, he'd chosen a full featured smart phone over a cheap underpowered laptop and he rarely regretted the decision. But sometimes a laptop was better for some things. He switched to his account on her machine and walked it over to the table.

Shortly, he had a private copy of the launch images of his own. He unplugged the USB cable and walked back to the bedroom. Propped so Biz wouldn't see what he was doing if she walked in, he began viewing the images again, at his own pace.

He got to where the probe approached the aurora lights when he heard the bathroom door open. Hurriedly, he logged out of his account and set the laptop on top of his backpack.

Biz walked around, turning out the lights in the common rooms and by the time she entered, he'd burrowed under the covers on his bed. She said nothing more and went to sleep.

Maybe he dozed, but when he woke, it was still dark. Biz was dead to the world and making those noises he claimed were snores, but she denied.

From her wisdom of elder sisterhood, she'd often told him that even if he couldn't sleep, he should just rest quietly because he would get a lot more benefit out of a half-sleep than he expected. Honestly, he tried, for maybe an hour. But his thoughts kept circling around the same issues over and over.

Biz liked Terry, and whatever flaws the guy might have, she couldn't see them. Whether it was some kind of reaction after her boss had betrayed her, or maybe she just liked the way he designed circuits, either way, Rule Six made a formidable barrier against his instinct to get out of Canada as fast as possible.

Not that he really believed Terry's club was some kind of spy ring, or terrorist group intent on lobbing bombs into the USA. His problem was that he had no idea who they were. He didn't have any clue as to their motives, or their capabilities. They didn't have to be some group out of a techo-thriller. There were some street gangs back home with no technology beyond a knife and no power beyond their own street. And yet they were lethally dangerous to anyone in the wrong place at the wrong time.

And then there was Sarah.

She was pretty, his age, and he'd really liked her online. She was just the kind of person he could trust, and had trusted. And unlike Donna, she didn't need any urging to dive into the cyber life. But she had lied, and was still hiding some deep dark secret.

What kind of secret could a group of kids be hiding, kids still concerned about their parents getting mad at them for being up too late at night?

It was useless. He wasn't going to get any more sleep. He pulled the covers aside and listening carefully for any change in Biz's breathing, he picked up the laptop and its charging cord and crept out.

He took it to the table and plugged in.

If I could get a really good look at the insides of the cylinder, maybe I could tell something more. Unfortunately, since he didn't want to turn on the lights, and the laptop's screen was too far away to provide illumination while it was charging, he was going to have to go out to the pickup and get a flashlight.

The floors were wooden and tended to creak as he walked, but there was no hope for it. He kept near the walls, hoping that he'd be nearer the supports that way and make less noise.

In spite of the street lights, he could see the Big Dipper high in the sky. They had come north, and it was plain to see in the positions of the stars. He really wanted to get out of town, at least down the road a few miles to shake free of the glare. On a clear night like this, the stars ought to be spectacular.

Oh. No sooner had he formed the thought of borrowing the pickup to go see the dark skies, than he saw the left front tire flat on the ground. The light caught a gleam off the valve stem threads.

They did that. I always leave the stem cap in place. He'd checked the air back at Baie-Comeau and everything was in place. The clean threads after hundreds of kilometers of dirt road was proof enough. They didn't want any escape in the dead of night and made sure of it.

Irritation doubled, he rummaged until he found a flashlight and checked that the beam was bright. It was chilly, so he headed back inside. There was nothing he could do about the tire right now anyway.

The laptop showed a very faint Wi-Fi signal, probably from one of the nearby houses. Unfortunately, it was too weak to establish a connection. He couldn't even tell if it was password protected. No chance of getting an alert out tonight.

Peering into the mangled insides of the cylinder gave him no particular insight. It was obviously home constructed, rather than some factory unit. Terry had spent a lot of effort putting it together. That indicated he wasn't government, didn't it? He wished he could be sure. Some time in the next day or so, he might have a window of time to make a call for help. If they were criminals, he could call the police. If they were government, that might be the worst thing he could do.

He went back to the photos. They were indeed a puzzle. A closer look showed details he'd missed before. The launch had been from next to a power transmission line, just like those they'd seen all along the highway. There was indeed no rocket glare. He should have been able to see it on the trees and hills, but there was nothing more than the utility lights he'd seen before.

That green light was a real life aurora, just like Biz had always wanted to see. He wanted to see it too. If he found out that there'd been aurora showing while he was in Canada, but he'd missed it because of the street lights, he'd be very upset.

The camera had picked up star images through the green glow. Could he, with a star mapping program, confirm the time and location of the launch? The moon was showing. That would let him nail down the day. It would at least let him confirm that the launch was the same night the cylinder crashed into his tree.

But one image, right before the spinning began, caused him to stop and zoom in. There was a streak of light like a meteor. Furiously, he looked for more streaks. And there were, lots of them.

Chapter 12: Unknown Secret

It was dawn before the old red pickup drove up. With the northern daylight schedule he'd woken from his fitful sleep much too early at first light. Through the window, he could see that it was the same one he'd seen last night.

"Biz! Terry is here." He heard her scamper over to the bathroom, probably to brush her hair or something. He went to the entryway.

"Good morning, Seth."

He nodded, not feeling cheery enough to return the man's smile. "Morning." It was hardly good. "Biz'll be out in a minute."

Was this a good time to ask questions? There were so many, he didn't know where to start.

Biz came out, all smiles.

"Terry. Good to see you, I just woke up a few minutes ago."

He held up a sack. "I brought bacon, eggs and tea, if you haven't had breakfast yet."

Tea? But Seth said nothing. It must be a Canada thing. But his chance for a man to man talk with his sister's new boyfriend was long gone. They didn't even notice he was in the room.

They made space on the table for the food by carefully shifting the cylinder and its attached wires to one end. Seth sat with them. The warm breakfast even produced a positive feeling or two in Terry's direction. He sipped the hot tea. With lots of sugar, it wasn't too bad.

The food was quickly devoured, but even before Biz had finished her eggs, she wiped her fingers and began poking at the wires. Terry did the same and it fell to him to clean up the residue of the meal.

As the two of them were digging into the broken GPS circuitry, Seth heard a mechanical noise outside. He raced to the door.

KC was pumping up his truck's flat tire.

"Hey!"

The boy jerked. "Sorry. I noticed you had a flat tire and I thought I'd just pump it up."

"Yeah! You let the air out last night. Afraid we'd escape." KC's look of guilt was plain to read.

Terry came out just in time to hear the accusation.

"Kolton, is that true?"

"Well, sort of. I just thought..."

Terry sighed. Biz was watching with a perplexed look on her face.

"Biz, Seth, I'm sorry this happened. It's true we were worried about you. Our probe was launched in secret and we could get in trouble if it got out on the Internet. But we're not going to try to keep you from leaving. We are grateful you spent the effort to find us. Getting some real numbers will make our project all that much more valuable."

Biz nodded, but she wasn't smiling. "Okay, let's get you your numbers. Seth, why don't you go back to the Town Centre and let your twitter friends know we're okay here, and exactly where we are. But keep Terry's project a secret."

Terry wasn't happy either. "Kolton, get that tire pumped back up, and don't let me see you trying something like that again.

"Seth, are you content with keeping our secret for now?"

He looked at Biz and Terry. It was a half trust. He could live with that for now. "I'll keep your secret."

They went back to the GPS. Seth packed up the laptop and charger into his backpack. KC was gone and the tire was refilled by the time he came back outside, but it really was just a short walk, so he didn't even try driving.

Sarah entered the door at the complex while he was still a few hundred yards away. He suspected she had been sent to watch over him. By the time he'd entered, she was nowhere to be seen.

The seats by the entrance, where he'd parked himself last night were already taken by some older men. They looked like truck drivers or construction workers; rough hands, coveralls and whiskers. Taking a morning break before heading out.

He needed a place to set up. Sarah went someplace and she was probably on line to check his tweets. It probably wouldn't hurt to watch her as she watched him.

Off to the left, the grocery store was doing business.

Bananas. Do they truck them in, or do they come by plane? He tried to imagine the shipping times for perishable items like fruit. From the way people talked, Goose Bay was a big city. Maybe produce was shipped in or flown in there and then trucked to Churchill Falls. Was Labrador City big enough to be a shipping terminal? They did have a Walmart.

It occurred to him that this little town in the middle of nowhere had a lot of nice facilities. What kind of a town was it?

On the second floor, there was a glassed in library, and Sarah was seated in front of a computer. She looked startled, for just an instant, and then waved.

Caught her at it.

He found a chair across the room and set up the laptop. Network popped up.

...

There was no sign that SaraCme had posted since yesterday.

SethPartner	Sitting in the Churchill Falls Public Library. It's part of this Town Cent(re) complex they have here. Grocery store is downstairs.
nickyWhy	@SethPartner So they got British spellings for stuff?

 SethPartner	@nickyWhy Yep. But it's sooooo much better than having all the signs in French. I can live with a little local colour.
 ClaraN1	Anyone seen @SaraCme? I was going to invite her to tackle the Celtic Grove. Seth? She usually asks about you.

Seth looked over at Sarah's red hair and watched her react. Yes, she was watching the tweets as well.

 SethPartner	@claraN1 I haven't seen her online since yesterday. But I have a feeling she'd excel at Celtic Grove.

He was right! She flushed and glared at him. On twitter, unless you used a self photo as your avatar icon, no one had a clue what you looked like. The gang had all gotten cartoon figures for icons, and SaraCme had followed the style, so no one knew what she really looked like. *Nobody but me.* Around this town there were enough people with red hair and names like Kelly that he suspected she had more than a little Celtic blood in her.

 moosenine	@SethPartner Hey bud. When you coming home?

 SethPartner	@moosenine Biz and I have to track down our mystery spot. It's close, but not on the road. Have to get a local guide. Can't abandon quest.
 moosenine	@SethPartner Don't forget my moose.

Seth looked over at Sarah. She looked up. He gestured at his screen and wiggled his fingers, pointing to her. *Are you going to post?*

She shook her head and looked back at her screen.

Probably wouldn't know what to say, now that I'm watching.

He was sorely tempted to post a private message to Nick, one where she couldn't see it, explaining everything.

But Nick just might reply openly. And he'd promised to protect their secret.

Although, I don't know what this stupid secret is! How can they expect me to protect it if they won't tell me what it is?

But there might be a compromise. He switched to the private message mode and posted.

 SethPartner	Nick, we had a flat tire this morning. I think we'll be okay, but if I drop off the radar for more than a day, you need to do the 911.
 nickyWhy	Sure. No prob. Any hottage between you and Sara?

| | Not very likely. But keep my worries from the girls. No real danger. I'm just being careful. Taking care of my sister and all. |
| SethPartner | |

When Seth closed the laptop, Sarah got up and walked over and settled into a chair close to him.

"Tell me about Moose. What is he really like?"

It was hardly what he'd expected her to say. Had his earlier gripe about her tweets to Moose hit home?

"Well, he's big. He's a defensive end in football. American football, not the other kind."

He told her a couple of stories about the big, kind-hearted Warrior and his habit of showing up with a new girlfriend practically every game.

"I know a guy like that." The conversation drifted over to Thunderbirds and Ice Cats and Huskies and the sport schedules of a small town where the nearest teams to play were over 200 kilometers away.

"Okay, I actually know what a Thunderbird is, the giant bird of Indian legends. Huskies are sled dogs. But what's an Ice Cat?"

"Well, Ice Cats are the girls hockey league. I'm on it." She grinned, "I'm also on the Thunderbirds, the boys hockey league. Small towns. You make do."

He laughed. "Now you really would impress Moose. Anything related to sports would get his undivided attention. TV is a box for showing sports to him, and nothing else."

Suddenly, KC rushed in. "The Army's back!"

The librarian, who had been calmly sitting at her desk in spite of their conversation, said, "Kolton! Be quiet."

Sarah grabbed Seth's arm and whispered, "Pack up your laptop. We've got to get back to the lodge!"

...

With two places to stay in Churchill Falls, and all the rooms in Town Centre taken, the overflow went to the Black Spruce Lodge.

KC talked as they walked. "Two trucks rolled in from Goose Bay. They asked for a place to stay overnight. I called Terry to warn him, but they're probably there already."

There was one military style truck parked at the lodge, with a Canadian Air Force decal on the side. Terry and Biz were standing on the porch, talking, while soldiers were moving in and out. When he saw them coming, about a block away, he gestured for them to slow down.

Sarah stopped, putting her hand on KC's arm. "Let's wait. Terry's got it covered for now."

Seth turned to them. "Tell me what's going on."

Sarah looked at KC hesitantly, then said, "When we launched the cylinder, some soldiers showed up the next day and walked around town, asking people if they'd 'seen anything'. Nobody knew what they were talking about and they left the day after. Now, they're back, and I don't know what that means."

"I've got to get back to the gas station." KC headed off at a trot.

I could blow this whole thing sky high. Just walk in and talk to the soldiers.

But did he have any reason to do so? He had promised to keep their secret. But was that enough?

The men in uniform had been carrying duffels into the lodge, and it looked like they were now loading up into the truck.

He turned to Sarah. "Give me a reason to stay quiet. I need to know what I'm protecting."

She sighed. "Okay, I'll see what I can do. Only be patient. I can't decide this all by myself."

When Terry and Biz got into Terry's truck and drove off, Sarah said, "I need to go check on something. Will you be okay for a bit?"

"Yes, I'll be quiet, for now."

When she left, he hefted his backpack and went into the lodge.

Two soldiers were resting at the table. They nodded when he entered and shed his shoes.

"Hi. Are you our new neighbors? We're in room four."

They nodded, to acknowledge his existence, but they were in a conversation of their own.

"I don't like helicopters anyway. Especially those civilian ones. Let the Chief have his inspection tour. I'll take the break and be grateful."

Seth went into the bedroom and closed the door. A quick check showed no sign of the cylinder or tool kits. Biz and Terry had obviously managed to smuggle it out to the truck before the soldiers had arrived. So, they were likely to be off somewhere working on it for a while.

He flipped open the laptop and then closed it again. This was not the place to be examining the photos, not when soldiers were moving in and out. Maybe they didn't suspect him of anything, but if they were in Churchill Falls to hunt for something related to Terry's club, then it was worrisome that they had arrived right when strangers from California showed up.

Part of him just wanted to put it all behind him. His paranoia was irrational and the club was nothing more significant than any other high school science club.

No, that's not true. These guys built a probe that went into space. That's a lot more significant than the thunder and smoke of my rocket launches. Maybe they are just a high school club, but I can't just sweep their accomplishment under the rug either.

He stretched out on the bed and closed his eyes. With just a couple of hours of sleep last night, he could use a rest.

Eyes closed, he kept seeing Biz and Terry chatting on the porch, Biz and Terry laughing over the electronics on the table, Biz and Terry comparing all time favorite breakfast meals as they ate bacon and eggs.

...

There was a knock on the door. Seth hopped up. It was KC.

A quick look showed no soldiers left in the common rooms. Had they left? "What's up?"

He looked nervous and uncomfortable. "Ah, I was sent to apologize about the tire. Sorry. It was my fault. I thought it was a good idea at the time."

"Good thing I noticed it before I tried to drive on it."

"Yeah." There was an uncomfortable pause. "My shift is over. I'm going down to the outflow. Do you want to do some fishing?"

Chapter 13: Fishing Revelations

KC was happy to show off his green Polaris Hawkeye 4-wheeler. "Get on." They roared off, heading toward the highway.

Seth leaned forward a little. "Where are we going?"

"Down to the river."

About a mile after the turnoff, Seth tapped KC on the shoulder and pointed to a big sign. He pulled off on the side of the road. The blue entranceway sign proclaimed Churchill Falls Generating Station and showed a numeric display showing the current number of megawatts being generated. As he watched it changed from 1926 to 2008.

"So, there is a power plant here. I thought there might be. Is there a dam near here?"

KC chuckled. "You didn't know? Everybody in town works for the company."

"I'm just a tourist, passing through. I saw the dried up falls."

"Yeah, sometimes, when the levees get full, the falls will get more water. But now, the water goes through tunnels from the lake over that way and empties out down at the river. The plant is underground. The largest underground hydroelectric power plant in the world."

Now that the subject had come up, Seth suddenly noticed all the power lines. There was a huge set heading off across the canyon, crossing the waterway several hundred feet below them. KC turned off the highway and followed the wide curvy path down to the water level. They pulled up near the outflow that spilled out from some tunnel. Overhead, the power lines stretched across the Churchill River, heading south.

"The water flow gets a lot bigger than this sometimes. It just depends on how much electricity they're making."

"When we were coming up from Québec, we saw lots of power lines like these."

KC twisted his face like he'd eaten a lemon. "Yes. Those go down and connect to the Hydro Québec system. There's a smaller transmission line that goes to Labrador City and the iron mine in Fermont."

"Iron! I saw that mine, but I didn't know what they were digging."

He laughed. "I saw Sarah's tweets. The vacant town was Gagnon. There was an iron mine near there years back. Then they moved to Fire Lake until it ran out of ore, too. That's when they picked up the whole town and moved to Fermont. I did a history report on it last year."

A curvy dirt road dropped the hundreds of feet down to the water's edge where KC had a nice wooden boat and fishing poles. "What are we fishing for?"

"Trout."

...

"They sent you to keep an eye on me, didn't they?"

KC chuckled as he cast. "No, actually. It was my idea. Like I said earlier. Sarah had been talking about you for days, and I saw a printout of her tweets. But I can't tell anything about people from a computer. That's her thing, not mine. If you can't make things blow up by pushing the joystick button, I'm not interested. I'm only in Terry's club to keep an eye out on her." He shrugged. "It was Dad's idea."

"Spying on your sister. My, my."

"Oh not really. Dad just wanted me to keep an eye on Terry, really."

"Oh? He has a dark past?"

"No. Everybody likes him. He grew up in Churchill Falls. That's what's so strange."

"Why is that?"

"Because he didn't leave."

Seth was puzzled. "I don't understand. Why should he leave?"

"Everybody does."

"Tourist here, remember. I know people back in Fresno that never left town their whole life. Born there, grew up there, got married and grew old, all within a few miles."

KC shook his head. "That's not how it works here. This is a company town. Everything's owned by the company, really. They hired Dad, and he moved here from St. Anthony, Newfoundland. The company owns the house. He says we have as good a school and stuff as we do, just to keep people like him happy.

"Kids like me grow up here, but we know that when we graduate, it's time to move on. Sarah will probably get a computer degree somewhere and leave. I know a few guys who have gotten jobs working on the Trans Labrador Highway. Maybe I'll do something like that. Probably, though, I'll go to Newfoundland. There's a lot more job opportunities there.

"Terry was one of the few who graduated and came back here to get a job with the company. Everybody knew he was smart and expected him to move to the big cities or go to the US. When he offered to start a science club, a bunch of girls joined, but I don't think they were interested in science, not like Sarah. But just about all of them quit once it turned out there was work involved."

"Why didn't he move on? Does he have family here?"

"Not any more. When his mother died, his dad went somewhere else when he graduated. I'm not sure where. Terry came back alone. Transmission line specialist. That came in handy."

"What do you mean?"

KC was suddenly interested in the water.

Seth reeled his own line in and cast again. KC had landed a five pound trout already, but all he'd gotten were nibbles.

"The fish in the lake get really big. We get tourists from all over who come to fish here."

Seth looked up overhead. "So...Terry works on those lines?"

KC could tell he wasn't going to be distracted by the fish. "Not exactly. There's all kinds of jobs related to the transmission lines. These are the 735 kilovolt lines to Québec. Most of the electricity goes there.

"The lines going towards Labrador City are 230 kv lines, and Terry works on the switchyard and those."

Seth looked up at the lines closer, seeing the huge insulators that had to isolate nearly three quarters of million volts. "I don't think I'd like working on something that would zap me."

KC chuckled. "Oh, it's not so bad if you just take the safety precautions. Once you guys started heading our way and people started getting all James Bond about the Aurora Launcher, we've gotten much more worried about being arrested than about the juice."

"Aurora? I thought your club had launched a rocket. What's this 'Aurora Launcher'?"

KC's eyes were wide and he gripped his pole tightly.

Seth pushed harder. "Come on. Tell me. You want me to keep your secret. I need to know what it is."

He had the feeling that if they weren't in the middle of the river, KC would have run for it. As it was, he was trapped.

"I'm not really interested in turning you guys in, you know. I just want to keep my sister safe. You can understand that, can't you?"

KC looked him in the eyes, and then nodded.

"Okay, but don't let on that I told you. I'd be in big trouble."

"I'll do what I can. But if you've got bodies buried in your bogs, all bets are off."

He gave one chuckle, but wasn't really amused by Seth's joke. "No, nothing like that." He reeled in his line.

"You see, it's the electricity. We've got a lot of it." KC waved at the lines, the rushing water of the outflow and everything around them. "We make it here, in Labrador, and then Québec takes it and resells it at a huge markup to the United States. We do the work and they get the profit."

"That doesn't seem fair."

"You don't know the half of it. When the agreement with Québec was made, they set the price at about a quarter-cent per kilowatt-hour. At the time, Québec held all the cards and we got stuck with a long term contract that doesn't run out for a few more decades, even though the cost of electricity has gone way up."

Seth nodded. He'd helped pay the bills at home. "My electric bill at home is like 50 to a 100 times that!"

"We make like two billion dollars worth of electricity a year here." He waved at the gushing water. "And make like three percent of it for the Newfoundland and Labrador economy while Québec rakes in the cash." He had an apologetic smile. "Dad gets riled up about it all the time, especially when his budget gets tight.

"So, anyway, Terry had this idea of how to use our excess energy in new ways–ways that could make the company money here, rather than just keep giving it away to Québec.

"Electricity is free here."

"Free?" Seth was shocked.

KC nodded. "Yes. None of the houses or buildings around here has a meter. The company owns all that, and it makes the electricity as well. I mean, Dad has a great woodworking shop in the back of the house and he makes furniture and gift trinkets and even this boat. He's running his saws and sanders and routers all the time, and all the electricity is free."

"And the street lamps, too."

"Yeah. All the lights. Everything. It just makes no sense to charge for that here."

Seth nodded, trying to get his head around the idea, remembering the household bills that included a significant expense to keep the air conditioner running in the summer.

"So, what did Terry do, build a rail gun or something to launch your cylinder?"

KC opened his mouth, then clamped it shut. "I can't tell you any more than that. I said too much already. You'll have to get the rest from Terry."

So, Terry and this science club have cobbled together some kind of electric launcher that lobbed an instrument package all the way to California. *That made sense. The cylinder never had an attached motor, if it was launched electrically. But how? Magnetism?*

"And now your group is afraid that the military is here looking for you?"

He sighed. "We don't know what to think! Out here, we hadn't any idea someone could notice what we did. How could they? But what other reason would there be for them to show up, twice!"

Seth pulled in his line. "Maybe we'd better go back."

•••

Two things raced through his head as they went back to shore and climbed the road back up to the highway.

What an amazing thing! Kids building some kind of space launcher out in the middle of nowhere. Just add unlimited electricity and boom—launch a camera so high it reached space and landed thousands of miles away. Reaching space with a home-brew project is the goal of all the model rocket clubs, even if we never say it out loud and even if we never quite believe it's possible.

But I've got to get Biz free of this Terry. Maybe he's a perfectly nice guy, even a genius. But with the military moving in, we have to be far, far away. We're foreigners. We can't be caught up in this.

We could even get in trouble with Washington, if they get the idea that we're involved in something strategically important and let it get away from us. Canada and the US have been friends, but they're two different countries with their own agendas.

I wish I could talk to the gang.

But for the first time, he realized he was caught up in something too dangerous to mention on the open Internet. He'd have to handle this by himself.

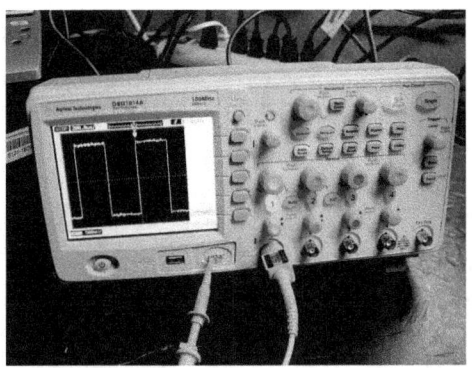

Chapter 14: Friends

The Black Spruce was deserted. The soldiers were gone, but a tin of shoe polish on the table was a sign that they were still in town, just off doing whatever they were here for.

I wish I dared check into their rooms. But that would be a bad move if I were caught.

KC was quiet as he looked around in the kitchen and laundry room, relieved that the soldiers were elsewhere.

"Do you know where Terry would have taken my sister?"

He shrugged. "There's only a few places. It's not a big town."

"Lead on. I need to talk to her."

"Um. How about the Teen Centre? The club meets there some times. It's just on the other side of the baseball field."

...

The plain, metal-sided building had guard rails outside the entrance, probably for stability when ice covered the walkway. As soon as they walked in, Sarah hopped up from her seat in front of the plasma TV screen, leaving the game controller at her feet. She looked at Seth and her brother. It was obvious KC was worried.

"Hi. I was wondering where you'd been to. Did you find out anything about the soldiers?"

Seth looked at the screen, where she'd been playing a first person shooter. The spaceship interior was still smoking from the flame thrower she'd been using, with pieces of her opponents littered over the ground.

"They're not there now. From what I overheard, they don't know what's going on either. Someone's doing a helicopter survey."

She looked alarmed, then turned to KC. "What are you doing? Terry emailed me. Something about letting air out of a tire?"

Seth held up his hand. "It's okay. He apologized."

"Yeah. Can I go now?" KC looked at Seth. He nodded.

He was quickly gone. The 4-wheeler roared off as if he were escaping the whole Canadian Air Force.

"What was that all about?"

Seth was tempted to tell her, and get more information about the Aurora Launcher, but he'd told KC he'd protect his source, so he just shrugged. "He took me fishing. Probably disgusted that I didn't catch anything."

She frowned. "To the lake or the river?"

"River, why?"

"He's gotten in trouble for taking Dad's skiff out into the current before. He's supposed to stick to shore fishing."

When he didn't volunteer any more information, she sighed. "Kids. Well, what do you think of the river?"

"Seriously, the canyon is pretty. A nice relief from the miles and miles of bogs and short trees. I also saw your power station. Two thousand and some megawatts."

"Oh, that's loafing. It'll do over five thousand, and they're planning additions downstream from here that will add even more."

Seth shook his head. "Do all you Churchill Falls guys know all the trivia questions about the power plant? I don't know a lot about the Fresno industries."

She chuckled. "Mom is one of the tour guides. She practices out loud sometimes. KC and I may have picked up a thing or two. Besides, I've been down inside with our Techsploration team. It's one of those 'get girls involved in tech jobs' school organizations."

Two guys walked in and dropped their jackets on the couch and went directly to the pool table.

Sarah gestured towards the door. He followed. The guys gave him a once over, checking out the stranger. The town was small, everyone knew everyone, at least in their own age group.

Outside, he asked, "Do you know where Terry could have taken my sister? KC was helping me look for her."

"Sure, let's check the Town Centre first."

It was close by. They walked the corridors on the first floor. No luck. The phone was in his pocket and he was tempted to connect, just to see what was going on, but he had to find Biz and he couldn't afford the distraction.

Upstairs, a man in a business suit walked out of the library as they approached.

"Oh, are you the California boy?"

"Uh, yes?"

"Good. I was going to have to go over to the Black Spruce and you've saved me a trip. It's you and your older sister, right?"

He nodded.

"Good, could you tell her to drop by the hotel here in the Centre sometime today?"

"Okay." And the man walked on his way.

He turned to Sarah, "Who was that?"

She shrugged. "Some guy in town administration. I don't remember his name."

"Well, one more reason to find Biz." They finished touring the Town Centre, with Sarah pointing out some of the places he might be interested in.

"Moose likes curling, I guess." He pointed at the entrance to the curling club.

"Does he play?"

Seth chuckled. "Not hardly. He's football, but he likes to watch nearly any sport. There's an ice skating rink in Fresno, Gateway. I guess the closest thing we have to curling is broomball, but that's just like hockey with regular shoes, and a nylon ball."

"So you've never tried curling?"

"No. Not something you see down in California."

"You need to try it sometime."

He shrugged. Not if he could get Biz out of town and out of danger.

...

"She's 'Elizabeth' isn't she?" They were walking down Lobstick Street, heading for Terry's house.

"Yes. But so was my mother. When I was growing up, she was occasionally called, 'Little Biz', but that faded over time. Besides, she's so business-like that the nickname fits."

"Your mother? Is she...?"

"Dead. Leukemia. We lost Dad to a roadside bomb in Iraq."

"Sorry."

"It's okay. We get by. I take care of Biz and she takes care of me."

"I got that impression from your tweets. When I discovered your account, I searched back in time for a year or so and tried to get a feel for what you were likely do to. You were always either fighting with her or taking care of her."

It was disturbing. For one thing, that all those casual thoughts of the moment were there on the Internet for anyone to research, and for another, that Biz made up so much of what he talked about. He always considered himself a pretty independent guy.

He griped, "Sorry I didn't try to spy out your history too."

"There wasn't any. I created the SaraCMe account just for this one purpose. I even used 'Sara' instead of 'Sarah' so it would look more American."

He chuckled. "I'd never have noticed one way or the other. I didn't even know Clara was black until she set up her new icon."

"You mean you aren't real-life friends?"

"Moose and Nick, yes. I've known them since forever. But Clara showed up as one of Moose's girl friends. I may have seen her at a football game, but I never learn the girls' names there. The fact that she was an online gamer was a bonus and who knows why she kept showing up on Twitter. Nick has a girl friend that looks like a model in one of those teen magazines, but Rebecca doesn't do Twitter at all, or if she does, Nick isn't sharing her ID."

"And you? Do you have a hidden girl friend?"

Donna, and a couple of other faces flickered through memory. "I have friends that are girls. No girlfriends." *Not anymore.* "A few that smile when I talk to them." He smiled at her, "You and Clara on Twitter."

Before she could react to that, he saw Terry's pickup parked at the next house. "Look. They're here."

...

At the step, he could hear Biz laughing. He started to knock, but Sarah just walked on in.

Terry looked up, oscilloscope probe in one hand, "Hello, Seth...Sarah." Something was still connected, because there was a square wave showing on the screen. Seth was familiar enough with electronics to know the distinctive look of a digital signal.

Biz turned part way to see them, but she had her hands deep in the circuits—the disassembled guts of the cylinder now spread out all over a workbench.

She nodded to Sarah, "Are you keeping my brother out of trouble?"

He was torn. It was good to hear Biz sounding as happy as she was, but he had to make the effort to keep her safe.

"Biz, we need to go."

She glared at him. "Not yet. Terry and I have a lot of work yet to do."

"Not leave town. But we've been asked to go over to the Town Centre for something."

"Who asked?"

"I don't know."

Terry joined in, "Sarah, what is this?"

"Yes, it's true. I don't remember his name. The man who gave the presentation on Nalcor history last fall?"

He nodded. "It's probably nothing serious."

Biz carefully extricated herself from the wiring. "Well, we'd better go see what it's all about."

"I'd be happy to come with you."

Seth was quick. "No. We can handle it. We've been taking care of ourselves for some time now."

He could feel the dark vibes from Biz, but she didn't contradict him. It was habit. Rule Three. No arguing in public. Don't give anyone any excuse to break them up.

Biz had the last word, "We'll be back soon. I want to be here to help swap out the controller."

...

The walk back was brisk. Sarah tagged behind a few paces. Seth whispered, "I've learned a little about what Terry's science club is doing, and it's probably illegal. We really need to get out of town before we get caught up in it."

She shook her head. "Terry has been open to me about the kind of thing he's been trying to achieve. I don't think there's anything to worry about."

"Did he tell you he's stealing power from his company?"

"He said it was irregular, but the company knows he's doing something interesting and is keeping its back turned."

"And you believe him?"

"Yes, I do. Now Rule Six. Leave it alone."

They were shortly at their destination. Biz walked up to the lady at the desk, "I'm Elizabeth Palmer, from California. I was told to come talk to you."

"Oh, yes." She grabbed up a clipboard with numerous names scribbled on it. "We have a bind. A group of soldiers came through unexpectedly and we're trying to juggle the available bed space. When you checked in at the Black Spruce, you didn't say how long you were staying. Have your travel plans settled any?"

Seth said, "We could leave. I think we've found out what we came for."

Biz shook her head. "But I promised Terry...Mr. Kelly that we would stay at least through Sunday. He invited us to attend church with him and I agreed."

Seth kept his mouth tightly shut, in deference to Rule Three, but he needed a serious talk, in private.

Sarah broke in. "Mrs. Jenkins, the Palmers came here to visit our science club. Internet friends, you understand. I bet I can find a place for them to stay in our homes. Would that help?"

She looked relieved. "Why yes, that would be lovely. If that is okay with the Palmers?"

Biz nodded.

"Good. Then why I don't I just leave that question mark by your room and if you would give me a call here if you can find them a place, I would greatly appreciate it."

Sarah shot him a look of glee, not realizing how trapped he felt. "Great, I'll go take care of it now."

Biz looked confident, daring him to complain. He said nothing, but something had to change.

Chapter 15: RV Guests

"We need to pack, no matter what last minute plans you've got up your sleeve," he whispered as they left the Centre.

They walked outside and started up the street towards the lodge side by side, not looking at each other.

"I don't know why you can't let me enjoy this visit! You're just determined to mess up the first good time I've had in ages. You have your friends, why can't you let me have mine?" Biz was steamed, but she kept her voice low.

"I've been working really hard to hold this all together and I thought you'd be happy for me. Terry is somebody I'd really like to know a lot better. We worked this out, Rule Six, remember. I think it's horrible how you just snipe, snipe, snipe. He's a good man, and I hate all these things you're accusing him of doing. I don't appreciate it one bit."

"Terry this, Terry that. I'm sick of it too. Go have your boyfriend. I don't care about that. But can't you wait until the soldiers are gone. He's into something dangerous. That's what KC and Sarah believe, and they probably know a lot more about this than whatever he's told you.

"Just *think* for a second, Biz. A missile landed in California from a *foreign country*. Yes, it was from Canada, a friendly country, but you can bet that if the Department of Homeland Security catches a whiff of this, that Terry and his club will be right up there on the terrorist watch list. They won't know that it's just your good and honorable boyfriend and a science club project gone wrong.

"General Whoever in Washington will call up his old Canadian Air Force drinking buddy in Ottawa and maybe they'll get the diplomats involved, but they won't wait on them. Something Unauthorized happened, and they'll want to put a stop to it as soon as possible."

"You're paranoid. Nothing like that is going to happen."

"Then why have the soldiers come? This is new. Ask Sarah."

Biz glanced back at their companion, but she was keeping a little bit back, and Seth suspected she was deliberately giving them some privacy. But when she saw that they were looking at her, she said, "I'll see you later. I've got to go arrange a place for you to stay."

"Thank you," Biz said. "I appreciate it."

"Not at all. Later." She turned on a cross street and was quickly out of sight.

The Black Spruce was a minute away, and neither of them felt like talking. They quickly got to business, packing up their bags. Biz folded the laundry she had done earlier and Seth took everything out to the pickup. Just as a precaution, he checked the tires and looked under the hood.

Parked next to him was a military truck. The soldiers were gone, but they'd left one of their transports. He couldn't see much of anything through the windows, not that he'd dare open the door to check closer.

Biz brought out her last bag and her coat. "That's all of it. I'm going back to Terry's place. Let me know if we have a place to spend the night."

He nodded. Neither of them had changed their opinions, but fighting wasn't any fun either. So, Rule Two. Biz was the 'parent'. She had the last word.

As he waited, standing beside the pickup, he noticed the other cars parked nearby. Some of them had power cords dangling out the front grill. While electric cars in a town where people didn't have any power meters made a lot of sense to him, he suspected the cords just went to heaters to keep the engines from freezing in cold weather.

The laptop was stacked on top of Biz's empty laundry sack. *Good. She didn't take it.* He got into the truck and opened the lid. The Wi-Fi indicator flickered. He had seen that before. Some of the houses probably had their own local networks. He tried to lock in a signal, but it wasn't strong enough.

He tried his phone, but it didn't see any signal at all.

No network, but he still had those photos to examine. The light streaks bothered him.

The military vehicle parked next to him kept him from opening the images. Not here. Not now.

...

Sarah appeared from around the corner. He waved, and she increased her pace. He reached across and opened the passenger side door for her. She sat down beside him in the pickup cab.

"Hi. I've got a place for you."

She gave him directions and he started the engine. No need to mention that he wasn't exactly legal to drive without Biz in the cab beside him. No chance in the world that a California Highway Patrol car would notice it here.

She directed him two blocks over.

"Park here, beside the RV."

Carefully, he pulled to a stop. A man came out the front door.

"Whose place is this?"

"Mine." She opened the door. "Dad, this is Seth!"

...

George Clarke was a mechanic at the generating station. "I make sure the water flows to the right places."

But he wasn't interested in talking about himself. After inviting Seth in, he wanted to know a few things about California, where Seth lived.

"No, it's not like the movies. There are gangs in Fresno, but it's not like I ever have to worry about them. We don't live in an area where the gangs frequent."

Mr. Clarke wasn't too interested in Biz, when he tried to talk about his sister. He only had questions about Seth and his life in Evil California.

I've got a bad feeling Sarah gave him the wrong impression about me. Did she overdo her 'Internet friend' story? Parents could be suspicious about that.

"I want to thank you again for putting us up. We didn't really plan this trip very well and our fallback position was sleeping bags in the back of the pickup."

"Mosquitoes this time of year would make it miserable. I don't even go visit my trapline cabin when it gets bad."

"Trapline?"

He nodded. "Mostly snowshoe hare." He got to his feet. "The RV will need some cleaning up. We'd better get started."

···

The first order of business was to plug the shoreline cable into the house outlet for electricity. "You can't drink the water. I haven't flushed the winterizing chemicals out of it yet, but it's safe enough for washing and flushing."

There was old trash to remove. Clothes and gear left on the couch, and a check of the fuel, water and battery levels.

There was a shortened queen-sized bed in the very back, and the couch folded out. "The table can be converted to a bed as well, but you probably won't need that."

Sarah was cheerfully unpacking the sheets and pillowcases. "KC gets the table bed on trips. He griped about it the whole trip to St. John's last summer."

"Where's that?"

Mr. Clarke chuckled. "Californian!"

She sighed at her father. "St. John's is on the island of Newfoundland. We took the Goose Bay ferry over. I had a queasy stomach the whole passage. We came back by way of Blanc Sablon and it wasn't nearly as bad."

He just shook his head. "I've never heard of any of these places. I'll just have to take your word for it."

She pointed at the laptop he'd brought in with the backpacks. "If you've got wireless on that, I'll show you on the net. The house Wi-Fi stretches out this far."

Her father opened the drapes on the side facing the house and said, "I'll leave the two of you to finish up. When will your sister get back?"

Sarah started, "Oh, I need to call Mr. Kelly and let her know where to come. I totally forgot."

"Well come on with me and get that done." He held the door for his daughter and escorted her out.

Seth unfolded the laptop and connected easily. There was no password.

···

There were several messages, as well as a private one from Nick.

nickyWhy	You've been 'off the radar' most of the day now. I keep checking and no word. I hope you answer soon, cause I don't know what to tell 9-1-1
SethPartner	I'm okay. It's been hectic today. Got kicked out of the place where we were staying by the Canadian military. We've moved to a loaner RV.

Nick must have had his twitter program open, because his reply came quickly.

nickyWhy	RV? moving up in the world. How's the search for the mystery spot?
SethPartner	Haven't nailed it yet, but I've talked to locals. On the right track. Pledged to secrecy. Tell you when I can. Keep this in the DM.
nickyWhy	Evil, evil. Okay, I'll keep it low, but I want full raw details soonest.

He switched back over to the public messages and tried to play catch up with the conversations that had moved on without him.

SethPartner	I've finally got Internet--stolen wifi from a house. Sorry I've been away all day.
SethPartner	@claraN1 I doubt I'll be anywhere near a console in time to play. It's pretty vacant up here.
SethPartner	@moosenine The locals tell me there are moose all over the place, but I have yet to see one in all these thousands of miles. Still looking.

Seth gave a twisted grin and typed:

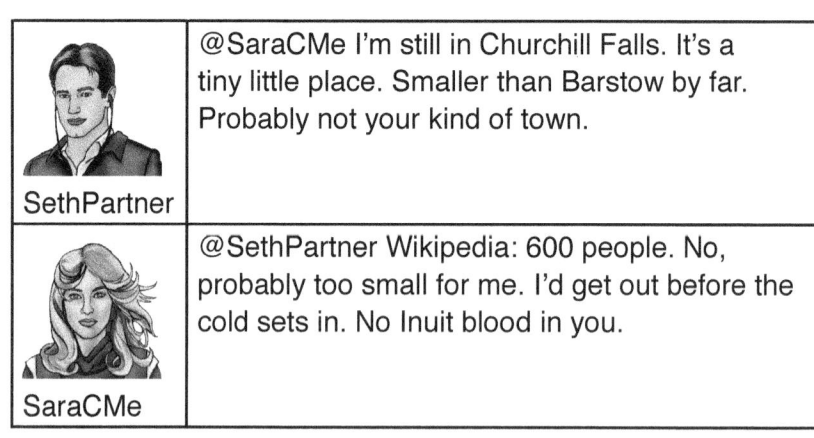

SethPartner	@SaraCMe I'm still in Churchill Falls. It's a tiny little place. Smaller than Barstow by far. Probably not your kind of town.
SaraCMe	@SethPartner Wikipedia: 600 people. No, probably too small for me. I'd get out before the cold sets in. No Inuit blood in you.

So, she was watching. He looked out the window. Behind a window in the house, he saw her hand wave.

nickyWhy	@SethPartner Wardriving in Labrador. Sounds like a good story.
SethPartner	@nickyWhy Pretty tame. No passwords. Too small a place to worry about them. I'd be surprised if the locals locked their doors.
SaraCMe	@SethPartner BTW, say hello to your sister for me.

Just about then, there was a knock on the RV door. He hopped up. Biz and Terry were at the door. She had another bag from the pickup.

"Come on up." He stepped back.

Biz climbed the steps, looked around at the interior and nodded. "This is really nice."

It wasn't five minutes later before Mr. Clarke and Sarah came out and it was a bit crowded, Seth sat at the table and closed the laptop. Sarah's father gave Biz the tour of the place. Terry sat down across the table and spoke in a low voice, "Biz and I are close to getting the GPS working again. It looks like some of the trajectory information is still in memory."

"Some of it?"

"I didn't expect anything more. Commercial GPS units are crippled by law. They're supposed to stop working if traveling over 60,000 feet altitude and 1000 knots." He grinned, "I think we exceeded both."

Seth had to agree, from what he saw in the photos. Biz asked questions about the RV's battery system and the inverters, things they as guests would never need to know, but she was that kind of person. Luckily, George was like minded and was happy to show it off. Unfortunately, that meant Seth had to get up off his seat, because the inverter was housed underneath it.

Sarah chuckled, "Looks like your sister is in the market."

He nodded. If they just had the money, it wouldn't be so bad touring about in a vehicle with a mattress, a heater, and electricity. Not to mention a bathroom and a shower.

His tour done, and his guests settled in, Mr. Clarke left and took Sarah along with him.

Terry said, "We still have a couple of hours work to unload the GPS. Do you want to come help?"

Seth shook his head. "I have things to do here. I'll see you later." He tried to smile and be friendly to the man. He had nothing against him personally.

Soon, he had the place to himself again. Surprisingly, it was already easing on down towards evening. Other than some jerky snacks KC had shared when they were fishing, he'd had little to eat. It was time to raid the ice chest.

...

Having Internet was a relief. He exchanged a couple of messages, but spent most of his time researching Labrador. Google Earth was a big disappointment. Off in the middle of nowhere, the satellite photos were of very poor quality. He could barely make out the town. He could see the path of the transmission line systems that KC had told him about, but there was nothing that could be seen off in the direction where the GPS had pointed. Even if there had been a Cape Canaveral launching tower hidden there, it wouldn't have shown up. Quite a contrast from what he was used to seeing in California, where individual cars and trees were plainly visible.

Wikipedia gave an interesting overview of the Canadian Air Force and he was intrigued by the NORAD connection. What little he knew about this radar detection system set up to detect ICBM attacks from Russia back in the old days seemed to indicate an interesting hole in its capabilities. The article talked about coastal radar systems. Did that mean that the radar shield looking for incoming missiles was aimed outward from systems on the coastline? If so, did that mean that a little missile launched from the interior of Canada and coming down in California might just be missed by the international alert system that America had relied on since the dawn of the Cold War?

Seth shook his head and blinked aside the fatigue that had come with the fading of the sunlight. He turned his search engine towards the sport of curling.

Chapter 16: Ballistics

The familiar engine sound of a 4-wheeler startled Seth awake just before there was a knock on the RV door. It was Sarah.

"Put on your coat. I just had a call to bring you over to Terry's house."

"Okay. What time is it?"

"Late. Dad was irritated by the call, but I got permission to take you over so you won't get lost. Let's go."

He climbed on behind her. He sat a little closer than he had when KC had driven him around. The air was cool and his arms around her waist were nice. She didn't say anything.

KC drove it a lot faster than Sarah did, but he suspected she was trying to keep the engine noise down. Churchill Falls had gone to bed and there were very few house lights on.

Sarah opened the door without knocking and the Terry and Biz looked up from the screen where they were examining a spreadsheet.

"Oh, good. There you are." Terry went right to the point. "Seth, what time of day did the cylinder hit the ground?"

"Uh...at night."

"Do you remember when, exactly. Did you look at a clock?"

He shook his head. "It was the middle of the night. No light out at all."

"So, after the moon had set, then?"

He struggled to remember. "I guess. Why? What's the problem?"

Biz explained, "We were able to tap into the GPS tracking record, but it shut down early in the flight, while it was still accelerating. It might have turned back on when it landed, but the impact made it switch modes and it didn't even record our road trip. I guess that's lucky because it might have overwritten the early data. I remember waking up when it hit, but I didn't check the clock. I was hoping you did."

Terry added, "The thing is, I don't know what the maximum velocity was. It took off here, and landed in California a few hours later. If it went nearly straight up with a little southern drift, it might have gone very high, perhaps thousands of miles high, and then crashed down four hours later when California had rotated into position. If it hit earlier than that, then the ballistic path was much more tilted towards the west, with much less energy. It could make a big difference in calculating just how fast it went."

Seth nodded, getting it. "Why didn't you put a radio transmitter in it, so you could track it in flight?"

Terry shrugged. "We did, but it burned out." He pointed at the disassembled parts on the table.

Seth moved closer to look. There was an antenna with carbon scoring. It had shorted out against the case.

"Wow, you must have had a lightning strike or something."

Terry made no comment. There were other possibilities, especially with some kind of electrically powered launcher and a probe that passed through the aurora. It was telling that he didn't mention any of that.

Does Biz know the whole story? If so, was she keeping it from him? He felt betrayed.

"It's past midnight. I think I need to go back to sleep, and Sarah has to get back so her father won't get upset with her. Sis, you need to rest, too. You've been at this all day."

She glanced at Terry, "You're right. I still have some work to finish up for now. I'll be there later."

Seth decided not to push it. "Is there anything more you wanted, while I'm here?"

Terry shook his head, "No, unless you happen to have an equation for calculating a ballistic trajectory when it's so high that you have to factor in the reduced gravity. It's not in my physics text and that's not my area of expertise."

"Sorry. I think I could do cannon ball stuff."

He nodded, "Me too, but once it gets really high, you need a more general solution."

Seth felt a pang of sympathy. If Terry was seriously considering a four-hour flight time, then it had to be very unusual. You could circle the earth in orbit in only 90 minutes, but what if you had no sideways velocity? He was used to rockets that just went up and then straight down, but in a matter of seconds. If you had a really powerful rocket, you could reach escape velocity and it would never come back. But if it wasn't quite that powerful, then it would come back down, perhaps much later. And what if the earth had rotated during that time?

This was totally different from all the textbook ballistics he'd ever seen. Usually it was just lobbing cannon balls over the next hill, or else adding sideways velocity to push your satellite into an orbit. No wonder Terry wasn't finding a quick equation to solve his problem. You'd have to be a real physics geek to work that out, and orbital mechanics wasn't Terry's field either.

"Okay, I guess we're going then. Sorry I couldn't give you a better time...."

He stopped, lost in thought.

Biz asked, "Seth? A problem?"

He blinked. "You know, I think I tweeted it, just a few seconds after the cylinder hit the tree. If we could pull up a log of my past tweets..."

Sarah moved over to a computer. "Already on it." Her fingers were flying as she brought up a web browser and searched for his twitter id. A few more screens and she'd scrolled back in time nearly two weeks.

"There it is. 2:12:33 am Pacific Daylight Standard Time."

Terry was scribbling it down. "Great. Once I get the equation worked out, this will be very useful."

Seth grinned at his sister. "And you said Twitter wasn't good for anything in the real world."

...

On the way back, he leaned forward and asked in Sarah's ear, "Is Terry a good guy? Biz is the only family I've got."

She slowed down and nodded. "Yeah. He's trustworthy around girls, if that's what you mean. When he started the science club, several of the senior girls joined just to spend more time with him. He wasn't that much older than they were. But they dropped out when he was oh-so perfectly formal around them. He's never spent this much time alone with any girl. Not even me, and I'm the only girl left in the club."

Seth didn't know whether that reassured him or not. Was it good that Terry was proper around younger girls, but didn't have any problem with being alone with his sister all day long and most of the night?

Sarah dropped him off at the RV.

"Do you want to come in?"

"I can't. Not here. I'm sure Dad is watching."

Seth glanced at the darkened windows of the house, but Sarah probably knew her family. "See you tomorrow, err...in the morning, then."

Biz arrived thirty minutes later, driven by Terry. They spent twenty minutes whispering outside the door before she came in. He wondered what Sarah's father was seeing, but he dared not spy on her himself. She'd catch him.

When Terry's pickup rumbled away, he asked, "What did you find out?"

The mystery that brought them all the way to Labrador was fair game, even if griping about Terry wasn't.

She sat down and logged onto her laptop. "I've got to check my email. Hang on a second."

He pulled out one of the powdered hot-chocolate mix packets and used the RV's microwave to nuke some bottled water. He remembered Mr. Clarke's warning about the water tap just in time.

Biz closed the laptop. "Well, you know the most of it. Terry and his band of helpers launched a rocket that landed in our back yard. He's now struggling to get all the data he can from the busted instruments. It's been quite a jigsaw puzzle, trying to coax data out of a circuit that by all rights should have gone straight to the trash."

Seth poured her a cup of hot water and she began stirring her own chocolate powder into it. He sat down across from her and spilled some of his own thoughts.

"Two things I've noticed. It wasn't a rocket. I saw the pictures and there was no glare from a rocket launch. A rocket that powerful, even a little rocket engine, would have lit up the countryside and there's no sign of it.

"KC stumbled and called it an 'Aurora Launcher', but I still don't know what that is.

"Second thing. They were all frightened to death that the military was coming for them. Whatever their launcher is, it's secret and not authorized. I know that in California, all big launches had to be certified. This is Canada, but I looked up the Tripoli Rocket Association website and they have Canadian chapters too, so probably similar rules apply here. Whatever they've done, rocket or not, it's not authorized and they know it."

Biz nodded. "An Aurora Launcher, eh? Sounds interesting. Terry had been very generic about his descriptions. I can use that."

"You haven't pushed for more explanation?" He was secretly relieved. His sister hadn't been hiding it from him.

"No. I was having too much fun." She blushed and looked down into her chocolate.

"By the way, dress better tomorrow. It's Sunday and we're visiting church."

"Why? It's Labrador." Seth was content with regular Sunday services in Fresno, but always felt a little uncomfortable when visiting other places.

"We went to church in Crescent City. Why not see what it's like here? I didn't make us stop when we were driving through South Dakota, but we know people here. Besides, I've already promised. We can leave Monday. I won't drag this out forever." She sounded a little wistful about it.

Seth felt guilty about taking her away from her new boyfriend, but with this concession to leave soon, he didn't want to make any waves.

Just let us get back into the United States and then she can spend all the time on line she wants with him.

Just let us get out of this mess safely.

Chapter 17: Paranoid

It was a small group. Churchill Falls a small town, but it wasn't as if everyone grew up in the same church that their ancestors attended, like some other small places. This was a company town, and it attracted skilled workers from all over. New people from differing backgrounds were arriving every year and efforts were made to accommodate their religious backgrounds. When Terry walked over to the church building with them, services were just letting out for a different denomination that used the same building.

By the time the twenty or so people gathered for the service, Terry had introduced Biz and Seth to nearly all of them and he had to answer the same questions about California over and over again. Seth started to notice a particular way, a speculative one, that people were looking at Terry and Biz. Then they asked, "How long have you known Terry? Did your sister meet him in college?"

He was relieved when the service started, and comforted that the first songs were ones he was familiar with. Unfortunately, sitting quietly during the sermon, with two days of little sleep, he dozed. When he abruptly woke up, nobody was looking at him, so he hoped he hadn't snored or anything, but he tried to stay awake for the remainder of the service.

The church building was on the same large lot as Town Centre so the walk to the Midway Restaurant for lunch was just a few steps. As they sat down to eat, Seth was feeling more and more like an unwanted tag-along. Not that Biz and Terry said anything to him, but that was because they were focused on each other, deep in a conversation he could barely follow. Biz had not only found someone she could talk to, but someone who actually spoke her language.

"Ah, the Palmers. I'm glad I saw you. How are you enjoying your stay here?" It was the lady who had been juggling the available rooms yesterday.

"It's wonderful. You have a lovely town here." Biz smiled widely, gesturing around her.

Seth nodded, a little amused at his sister. She hadn't gotten out to see anything. He added his comment. "This is certainly one of the prettiest places we've seen in Labrador. I went down to the river yesterday."

She was genuinely pleased. "I'm so glad. Well, I've been told that the airport construction has gone well and most of the soldiers will be moving out this afternoon, so if you wanted to move back into the Black Spruce Lodge...."

Biz shook her head. "No, I think we'll be just fine where we are. Thank you anyway."

...

Sarah showed up in the doorway when he had barely started on his plate. He waved and she came over.

"I was hoping to find you here."

"Good news. The soldiers are moving on."

She sighed with a relief so visible that Biz noticed. His sister nodded slightly to him, recognizing what he'd been trying to tell her.

He picked up his plate and said, "Let's move to another table. These two have been ignoring me all morning." Everyone laughed, but there was no objection.

They chose a comfortable booth across the room. Sarah had already eaten, but she ordered some fries and gravy. She smiled and reached into her shoulder bag. "Guess what?"

"What?"

She produced an old Palm Pre. "My brother's. My older brother–he's moved to Winnipeg, but left this. It still works. She tapped on it with a stylus.

His phone beeped. He pulled it out. It had picked up the Town Centre Wi-Fi it had memorized before.

SaraCMe	@SethPartner Seth, are you still in Churchill Falls?
SethPartner	@SaraCMe Yes, in fact. I'm having lunch right now.
SaraCMe	@SethPartner What are you eating?
SethPartner	@SaraCMe Fish and Chips. Looks like battered cod and fries. Nice and greasy.
moosenine	@SethPartner Order me some of that. It's still early, but I haven't had breakfast.
ClaraN1	Ughh! You lost me at grease. Don't they have grilled fish there?

SethPartner	@claraN1 Probably. I only read part way down the menu and it sounded good.
moosenine	It does sound good.
ClaraN1	@moosenine I hate you guys that can eat that stuff and then go run it off on the field. I've got to watch what I eat.

Sarah laughed. "I think Clara is stuck on Moose. What do you think?"

He shrugged. "I don't know. What makes you think it?"

"She's always on line when he is. And didn't you say she was one of his girl friends."

"Yes, but so are you."

Biz and Terry got up from the table and left. They waved in passing.

ClaraN1	@SaraCMe back me up, girl. Tell these idiots to lay off the grease.
SaraCMe	@claraN1 I don't know. I do love a good plate of fries.

It was just one of those quirks of lighting, but by the double reflection off the picture glass and then the decorative separator above Sarah's head, he saw a familiar face. One of those soldiers he'd seen in the Black Spruce had settled down at a nearby table.

Sarah was tapping away, deep into her argument with Clara. Seth sat very straight, so he could get a better look at the man via the indirect view. He was in ordinary clothes, a plaid shirt and jeans, but it was definitely the same guy.

He tapped on his phone.

 SethPartner	I just saw someone, a soldier I met at the place I stayed the other night. Here in the restaurant. Gotta go. Talk at you later.

Sarah looked up from her tiny screen, with a puzzled look on her face. He gestured for her to stay calm with his right hand so the man couldn't see. She nodded.

 SaraCMe	@SethPartner Travelling the world and meeting new people, I see. Keep us updated. L8tr.
 ClaraN1	@SethPartner Yeah, be our tour guide. And if you can, join the game at about 2.

"I guess I'd better finish these before they get cold." Sarah spoke loud enough for the soldier to hear, if he were listening. "Would you like to go see our selection of games at the Teen Centre?"

"Yes, that would be good."

...

When they were well clear of the place and with no sign the soldier was following them, he asked, "Did you get a good look at him as we walked out?"

"Yes. He's definitely no one I've seen here in town before." Her face looked like there was a cloud over it.

"Do you think that he's actually watching us, or could it just be a coincidence. Maybe he's on leave or something."

She was chewing her thumbnail, then glanced hurriedly back at the Centre. "Oh, he wouldn't be watching you. You're just a tourist. You weren't even here when we launched, and if he's a spy, then he knows that."

"He's following me, I know it. I'm the one who faked information on Twitter and Facebook."

"Oh, calm down. You're just being paranoid."

She nodded vigorously, "Yes, but I have reason. I'm the one he sat down to spy on. I'm the one acting strangely. I'm the one committing fraud on the Internet."

Once safely hidden inside the Teen Centre, she calmed down a little. "Here, take a look at the games."

He perused the titles, and then thought about the carnage he'd seen on her screen the other time.

"How about let's play pool. I don't usually have access to a table."

She agreed, and soon the worry on her face was directed at lining up her shot, rather than at imagined spies.

...

Hours later, KC came bounding in just as Seth was proving to Sarah that although she could beat his pool skills 100% of the time, he was still able to checkmate her when it came to chess.

"The soldiers have just left. I pumped their tanks and they just drove off."

"Which direction?" he asked. He didn't want to ask if he'd seen all the military vehicles leave. That would just get her paranoid again.

"Labrador City. I heard them mention something about installing radios at Wabush Airport."

He nodded. "That's the same story that the hotel lady had. Airport construction. Do you think it could be true? Maybe they aren't looking for you guys at all."

Sarah asked, "But what about our spy?"

"What spy?"

Seth shook his head. "Don't worry. It's just some guy we saw at lunch."

"It was a *soldier*, dressed in civilian clothes, spying on us in the restaurant!"

"We don't know that. And maybe he left with the others."

"Then why was he dressed in civvies?"

Seth wanted to believe everything was okay. He wanted it to be a false alarm. But what if Sarah's worries were more than just paranoia?

KC said, "Why don't we check?"

"Check what?"

"Let's go to the airport and see if they've added anything."

Seth looked at Sarah. "What do you think?"

"Yes, but let's keep an eye out for our spy."

"Okay, we can take my truck." Seth offered, any chance to get more time behind the wheel.

"No, we'll drive. We know some shortcuts if someone's trying to follow us."

KC grinned. "Right. You stay here. Sarah and I will go get the 4-wheelers."

They left. Seth looked around the room and put the pool cues back on the rack. He was a guest here. He shouldn't leave the place trashed out.

...

They weren't long. Both showed up on nearly identical rides. Sarah's was blue instead of green, but they looked like the same model. He hopped on behind her. KC grinned at him and roared off toward the highway.

Seth enjoyed the ride, although he did look back behind them from time to time, searching for any sign that they were being followed. He was glad this stretch of the road was paved, or they'd be eating KC's dust.

This is the place Biz said was closest to the launcher. But there was still no sign of anything unusual and Sarah didn't slow down until they reached the turn-off for the airstrip.

They stopped near the main hangar and got off on foot.

"It looks pretty quiet here."

KC nodded. "We don't get a lot of traffic. So unless somebody wants to use the helicopter or a plane is scheduled to arrive, there's no real activity here."

There was a car, so someone was inside, but it was a pretty open place to walk around.

Sarah was peering up at the roof, where several antennas were showing. "I think that one is new, but I can't be sure. I haven't been out here in a while."

KC came around the back side of the building. "Hey, guys, come here."

In the dirt, near the antenna, he picked up some freshly stripped antenna coax. "Their cleanup must have missed this." All three of them looked up and sure enough, the color matched a fresh cable run from the building up to the antenna Sarah had thought was new.

"That's it then. The crew were here to install a new radio system. They weren't here to find your Aurora Launcher after all."

Sarah turned on her brother, "Kolton!"

Seth chuckled, "Don't blame him. I already knew you launched the cylinder with some kind of exotic launch system. The story that it was a model rocket was blown the instant I saw the pictures that Terry unloaded from the camera. It's some kind of electrical launch system and if Terry is trying to hide that from me, he's not doing a very good job of it."

Chapter 18: ISS

Sarah and KC were agreed that the first order of business was to tell Terry about the radio installation. If the soldiers were just a harmless distraction, he needed to know about it.

"We haven't used the launcher since they showed up the first time, and that was right after the cylinder went up. He was still tuning it."

Seth soaked up the words. Sarah may have assumed that KC told him more than he actually did, so he wasn't about to ask questions and destroy the illusion. *A tunable electric launcher.* He filed the information in the back of his head.

As they rode back to town, he thought about all the launcher ideas he'd ever read about. There were the laser launchers that used ground-based lasers to vaporize ice into a rocket exhaust, but that was ruled out by the same lack of glare in the photos.

There were linear accelerators. Those used a string of magnetic coils to pull a metal target faster and faster until it had the velocity it needed to reach space. Unfortunately, those designs were stretched out across the ground, or up the slope of a mountain. It would take a big expensive construction project, well beyond the means of a high school science club. And the photos showed the cylinder going straight up, not across the landscape.

Even with the clues he had, nothing yet made sense. The photos and the slips KC and Sarah made helped, but he needed more information from the inventor himself.

If it really works, what a wonderful breakthrough. Getting into space with electricity could really expand what can be done.

He loved a thundering blast of fire from a big launch as well as the next guy, but harnessing what was essentially a controlled explosion was always going to be under the thumb of a government wanting to keep its citizens safe.

It just seemed to him that an electric launcher, with no blast, and no toxic fumes to worry about, would have to be a safer system, and one that just might let people like him get involved in a real space launch. In spite of all his worries, the idea that he could be part of something like this kept nagging at him.

...

Terry's truck was parked at his house, but Sarah went in first and came right back out.

"They're not here."

KC looked at his watch. "They could have gone for dinner."

"Check the restaurant?" Seth asked.

They got back on the 4-wheelers and checked. No sign of them, and no one had seen them since lunch time.

"Could they have gone back to the RV?"

Back at the Clarke house, the pickup was still parked by the RV, but there was no one inside. Sarah checked in the house with no luck.

Seth sat down on the entrance steps of the RV. "Is there any place else he might have taken my sister?" It was starting to worry him. "Does he have an office at the power plant or somewhere in town?"

The street lights came on. Darkness had come to Churchill Falls.

"Not that I know of." Sarah leaned against her 4-wheeler.

"Where do you think he is?"

She looked at her brother. "There is one other place."

KC nodded. "The launcher."

Seth straightened up. "Yes. Biz was ready to pester him for more details last night. He was there when we heard that the military were moving out. He might have considered it safe enough.

"You have to take me there."

She looked up at the sky. He followed her gaze to the north. The street lights had already turned everything orange. If there were stars, they weren't bright enough yet.

"I'll need my coat. You will too. It gets chilly at night."

"I could take our pickup."

She shook her head. "It might not make it. We need the 4-wheelers. Hang on." She went into the house.

Seth reached into the RV and picked up his coat that he'd left on the couch next to the door. KC was already wearing a light jacket.

"Why do you have so many street lights?"

KC shrugged. "You've never lived here in the winter. Sunset is like 4PM and it feels like it's dark all the time. Street lights are just part of living here."

"Ah!" It finally made sense. People living this far north needed the lights. "I just like to see the stars at night."

He chuckled, "Oh, you'll see them soon enough."

Sarah came out, "Get on."

...

Almost as soon as they reached the highway, Seth began to see what KC meant. The street lights were everywhere in town, but that was just a tiny island of light and once they were half a mile down the road, the town was just an orange blotch on the horizon and the stars were out in their full glory.

The Big Dipper was much higher in the sky than he was used to.

"Hang on."

He held on to her a bit tighter, as she slowed and pulled off the highway onto a narrow dirt stretch. KC was right behind them. They dipped low and into a flowing creek. Almost before he tried to raise his shoes to keep from getting them splashed, they were across and climbing the other side.

He really had to hold on tight then, as the roadway was rough. Sarah revved the engine and sped up.

Power lines ahead showed where they were going. It was a maintenance road that followed the transmission line. The trees were gone. This was a passageway kept clear so no tree would grow tall enough to touch the high voltage wires.

What did KC say? Two hundred and some kilovolts. This is the route to Labrador City. We must have paralleled it the whole way driving here.

He wondered if the utility road went the whole way, or was it just here, close to the town.

It was dark, and getting darker. Low hills separated them from the Churchill Falls lights. With no smog and no cloud cover, he could barely see a glow over the blackness of the hilltop. With no moon, the headlights and the stars provided the only light.

Or maybe not. Off on the horizon to the other side, he could see a glow.

"What is that? The airport?"

She laughed. "No. Northern lights."

He wanted to stop right there and turn off the headlights. He'd never seen the aurora before, and he wanted to drink in the experience.

But they weren't to the launcher yet, and he really wanted to see that.

He kept his eyes on the glow in the sky, and he was sure it was moving. Was it the same color he'd seen in the photos? He couldn't tell. His eyes weren't pulling too much color out of this faint light. Were they getting closer? He hoped so.

"He's there." Sarah slowed down to a halt. KC moved up beside them. She turned her headlights off and then blinked them once before killing the engines. KC did the same thing.

"What's going on?" With the headlights off, the surrounding landscape was dead black, and the stars overhead blazed. Tiny stars he'd never seen before covered the sky–so many that it was hard to make out the main constellations for all the competition.

And the aurora was much brighter than he'd seen before. Yes, there was green, and it rippled in the sky.

"We have rules. We can't take the machines any closer than this. The headlight blink is to let Terry know that it's us. Otherwise he wouldn't turn the launcher on."

"The launcher is here?"

"Yes, can't you see it?" She took his hand and pointed it for him. Several hundred yards ahead of them in the middle of the clearing, there was a faint light on the ground.

It's the fence I saw in the pictures. It's glowing.

"Can you see him? Can you see my sister?"

"Not in this light, but since he's already started the cycle, we'll just have to wait here."

He shivered. Summer or not, he was cold. He zipped up his jacket, and pulled out the wool gloves he always kept in the pocket.

The power line hum, the same thing he'd heard back at the switchyard on the way up to Labrador, shifted a bit.

"Look," KC said, "It's starting."

Off to the right of the glowing fence line, nearly at the tree line, it appeared as if a large fifty foot tall water tank began to glow as well. Something fat and round was wrapped in lines, perhaps the coils of an electromagnet? But it was humming at a different, higher tone than the power lines. *It's magnetic! Even the 4-wheeler is vibrating.*

Together, the tank and the fence line began to shift brightness, linked together. Brighter and dimmer, irregularly, like they were struggling to match some other signal.

And overhead, he could see the aurora bands pulse too.

They're connecting! Has Terry figured a way to control the aurora?

They found their sync. Faster, the apparatus on the ground and the powerful glow overhead, powered by particle blasts from the sun's atmosphere, began flickering in a locked dance. Whatever the connection, it was getting stronger by the second. *Is it magnetic, all the way up to space?* The photos of the cylinder accelerating all the way up flickered in his head. *Yes!*

KC yelled, "Sarah. There's an airplane, to the southwest."

Seth turned and looked. Low on the horizon, an unblinking bright dot was headed their way. It seemed to be heading straight towards the flickering lights overhead.

A meteor streak, starting from overhead, flashed across the stars and vanished. Then there was another, fainter, but also starting at the zenith, heading in a different direction.

Seth looked back at the dot on the horizon. He recognized it. Horrid suspicion crashed over him. He had to stop the launcher!

"Sarah! Can you signal Terry to stop?"

"What? Why?"

"That's not an airplane. That's the ISS, the International Space Station. We have to stop the aurora machine right now!"

"We can't. Terry has the controls, and we're supposed to stay here."

There was no time to explain. He ran over to the nearest 4-wheeler and started it.

"No! Seth, no! You can't go any closer."

But he had to.

He revved the engine and before Sarah could reach him, he moved off. He had to reach Terry and stop this thing before the ISS could be affected.

Sarah screamed behind him. KC was yelling too.

In the headlights, he could see the little control shed a respectful distance from both the tower and the fence line. There were two dark figures silhouetted in front of the lit up trees.

It was the last thing he saw before the world flashed painfully bright.

Chapter 19: Zapped

"Huff!" The blow to his chest hurt! Was it Bud Jackson? *No. That was a long time ago.* He wasn't in Baird Middle School any more. He hadn't been beat up in years. But he ached all over, and when hands came down on his chest again, he struggled and tried to knock them away.

"Seth!" In the darkness, he looked up at Biz, her face half lit against the night sky. His eyes struggled to focus, and when they did, light above in the sky brought back the memory. The aurora blazed across the stars.

"Stop it! Turn it off." Even speaking hurt.

Terry put his hand on his shoulder to restrain him. "It's off! Everything's okay!"

"The aurora!"

"It's okay. It's glowing on its own. I may have triggered a brighter display, but the coil is off. I saw your headlights and I almost got it off in time, but not before you drove into the hazard zone. Why did you do something like that?"

"The ISS space station. It was coming. It was in danger."

Terry looked up into the sky, but the bright dot had already gone. He shook his head, "No. We're an easy two degrees north of the space station orbit's inclination. It never gets any closer than a few hundred kilometers to the south of Churchill Falls. I've observed it many times before, and I'm sure of that. We can see it from time to time, but it never gets very high in the sky. Besides, we weren't launching anything tonight. I was just showing the coils to Biz. She had never seen an aurora. And I knew this was the way to trigger one."

Seth sat up and put out his arm, trying to get up. The ground was cold and rocks dug into his backside. But he was still too unsteady.

"Just take your time. You took a considerable shock. If the ATV's metalwork hadn't taken the bulk of the hit, you'd be dead by now."

Seth could tell he didn't understand.

"Terry, it doesn't matter that you weren't launching. Didn't you see the meteors?"

Terry looked puzzled, and then nodded.

Seth rolled on his side. Every muscle ached, like from a leg cramp. Probably the electric charge had tied his whole body into a knot for an instant. He'd have bruises.

"Your launcher thingy makes a super magnetic field, right? That's how you launched the package?"

Terry put his arm under his and helped him to his feet. Seth had to hang on to keep from falling again.

"Yes, the coil on the ground syncs the aurora into a matching phase. The result is like a magnetic coil that runs all the way from the ground to a couple hundred kilometers high inside the aurora. It'll pluck anything metal right off the ground and accelerate it towards the center of the column, half way up. Ideally, we then turn off the coil once the probe reaches the middle. Momentum would take it even higher, all the way into space. We were trying to calibrate that timing with our GPS probe so we could get maximum efficiency."

Seth hobbled a couple of steps. And had to grab onto the handlebar of the 4-wheeler for stability. Biz was right by his side, ready to catch him if he fell.

"That's what makes it dangerous. It works both ways! Your magnetic field reaches up into space. Just like it pulls metal off the ground, it's also pulling satellites out of orbit! That's what those meteors are. Space junk, and maybe whole satellites. Every time you turn it on, anything that swings through the top side of the field will have its orbit disrupted. Maybe not a lot, but from those streaks, it's enough to pull some of them into the atmosphere. That's why I had to stop you when I saw the ISS. There are people up there."

Terry had his arms out on the other side, ready to help him as well, but when he heard that, they dropped and the light from the other 4-wheeler's headlights showed his mouth open and his eyes wide as he absorbed the idea that his launcher was more, much more than just a way to throw things upward.

"I didn't think...."

"And that's why the military is sniffing around..." Seth struggled to put into words the idea that had become clear to him, right before the massive electric zap tried to do him in. "Maybe they never saw the cylinder go up, but NORAD knows that something is disturbing the satellites. They track those things, even little fragments and lost wrenches in orbit. I'm sure their computers have already told them that something is happening when satellites swing over mid Labrador. How many times have you fired this thing up?"

"Four times, at least at this power. I had an earlier version that...never mind. It never formed the magnetic column."

There was silence as everyone tried to understand.

KC asked, "How much do satellites cost? Millions of dollars I bet. If we're knocking them down.... I saw the meteors too but I never thought that they were satellites."

Terry mumbled, "None of us did. I thought they were some high altitude effect of the aurora."

Seth held onto the handle bars and looked around at the launcher, partly visible in the light. The coil was just a simple fence line that faded away into the darkness. He sniffed. "Something smells."

Sarah sighed, and said, "Yes. It's my ATV. The wiring is fried. And maybe your hair. I don't think I'll ever forget the sight of you like a black cutout surrounded by the white lightning flash. I expected to find you black and smoking. But the juice must have shorted through the frame instead. Dad's gonna kill me when he sees it."

Biz took his arm. "We need to get you back into town and check you out." Her voice was shaking. She was angry, and didn't look Terry in the eyes.

There were three ATV's and one was toast, with five people.

KC said, "I'll stay here. Sarah can come back to help tow the other one."

Biz drove Seth, and Terry went with Sarah.

Seth suspected his sister was crying, but she was quiet about it. He expected her to yell at him for driving so close to the coils, but it never came.

The bouncy path back to the highway went slower with Biz driving than it had with Sarah, and every bounce reminded his aching muscles how stupid he'd been. Sarah and KC said they were stopped there for safety. He hadn't paid attention.

I could be dead now. Were they doing CPR on me? Had my heart stopped?

He shivered, and this time, not from the cold.

Once they got to the RV, she made him go into the enclosed bedroom at the rear and check himself out for burns. His left leg had a long streak down it, and his shoe had a hole burned through it. His gloves smelled like burned rubber where the handle grips had melted a little, and he wasn't sure he'd be wearing them again.

Biz raided the Clarke's medicine cabinet in the RV and found burn ointment. She applied it, and he saw that she was shaking as she did so.

"He should never have built that thing! It's criminal he let children get close to it."

Seth found himself defending the man.

"It is a great invention. I was warned about the safety range, but I didn't pay attention when I saw the space station. I guess I was thinking it was like a rocket's safety zone–just a precaution in case something catastrophic went wrong and the rocket blew up. This wasn't a just-in-case protective zone, but a you-will-get-zapped one. It's my fault for jumping in without knowing what I was doing."

She couldn't look him in the eye and he knew she was torn up about it, and probably more about Terry than about him.

"It will be better in the morning."

He hoped. The muscles still ached. "Do we have any aspirin?"

...

Sleep was hard coming. It was impossible to find a comfortable position, even if he turned on to his side so the worst of the burns didn't have any pressure on them. Muscles ached and twitched. And he had no peace.

I'll never get to be a part of this. Stupid and blundering in where I had no business going. I deserved to get fried. I can't help them, and whatever I do just causes disruption and destruction.

Sarah's ride. He shook his head. *Trashed it.*

And have I destroyed the dream as well?

Almost from the first moment that he understood what the launcher did, he imagined himself in a tiny metal capsule, with suitable safety gear of course, launched up into space.

Spaceflight was for elite soldiers and millionaires, and he had little chance of being either. But the dream had inspired garage engineers for decades to craft rockets with their limited resources that reached for space a few thousand feet at a time, knowing that gravity would always win.

But Terry and his group had gone so much farther. He was sure every one of them had dreamed of hitching a magnetic column into space itself where they could see the curve of the Earth below with their own eyes and feel the limitless stars within their grasp.

Had he killed that dream?

More than for her fried 4-wheeler, she could hate him for that.

...

It wasn't any better when Monday's morning light arrived.

Biz had slept on the couch and answered the door. It was Mr. Clarke, and he was upset about his fried 4-wheeler.

"We were just packing to leave. I'm really sorry about this."

Seth hurriedly slipped on his jeans and shirt and stumbled out.

"This is my fault."

Mr. Clarke's face was fixed and solemn. Without a word, it was plain he wanted an explanation.

"KC and Sarah were showing me around the town and I got too close to one of those transformers. They tried to warn me. It wasn't their fault at all. There was a spark of some kind and it fried the wiring."

He didn't quite believe the story, and Seth tried to keep it as simple as possible.

Biz jumped in. "Regardless of how it happened. I will pay for everything. Let me get my insurance card."

She dug out the numbers and promised that even if the insurance company wouldn't cover it, that she would make it good. He asked some questions about how he would be able to get in touch with them when they went back in the USA. There was some debate about whether to call the police in on it, since it wasn't actually a road accident, but Biz was persuasive and wrote him out an initial check for $1000 for repairs. Since it was just paint and wiring, that might cover it.

They promised to be out of the RV in an hour. He left to go to work.

She sighed after he was gone. "That was expensive."

"I'm sorry. How much does one of those things cost anyway?"

"I have no idea. But I had to do something. Now I'm just as paranoid as you are. I don't want anything on an official record. Not if we're part of a criminal conspiracy that might have caused millions of dollars in damages."

They loaded up everything into the pickup. Biz took an extra twenty minutes washing up all the counter tops and refolding the sheets and blankets.

Seth was outside, arranging things in the back of the pickup when he saw her working through the window. She was shaking. Then sobbing. All his good feeling from finally making their escape bled away. He finished up and then sat in the cab of the pickup, waiting for her to finish on her own time.

There were no sign of tears when she came out.

She sounded cheerful as she sat down at the steering wheel. "We already filled the gas tank when we arrived. Now, which way back? Retrace via Manic-Cinq and Montréal, or go on to Goose Valley and take one of the ferries out that way?"

Just putting it in words made it sound like a defeat, and he really hadn't expected to feel that way. Real life waited for him back in Fresno. The gang was waiting. He'd have stories to tell, and some of those were too dangerous for the internet. They had to wait until he was safely back home and could explain in person. Unfortunately, real life no longer had much appeal, not after what he'd seen here.

Coming here, the lure of the mystery spot and the freedom of being a tourist had brightened the days. It was different now. Just a couple of days ago, Goose Bay had sounded exotic, and Newfoundland called, but could they afford to linger in Canada if they were trying to leave the danger behind?

"Here comes Sarah and KC. Have you said your goodbyes yet?"

He looked up, feeling like he should hide. They had every reason to hate him. He'd crashed their 4-wheeler, and rubbed their faces in a serious problem with the Aurora Launcher. Part of him just wanted to get back on the road and avoid this.

"I'm glad I caught you. I hope Dad wasn't too unpleasant." Sarah looked worried.

KC grumbled. "Yeah, he gave us the royal lecture on the dangers of power lines, like he has a clue about what the club is doing."

"I told him it was all my fault. And I'm sorry your ride is zapped."

Sarah looked at the truck. "Are you leaving?"

Biz nodded. "We need to get back home, and now is as good a time as any. We've been gone far longer than we ever planned." Seth felt a tightness in his chest as she said it. It wasn't logical to stay, especially after all his efforts to leave, but part of him wished he could.

Sarah looked at Seth and said, "Well, we just got word that Terry is calling a meeting of the club at the Teen Centre. It would probably be a good idea if you came along. You two are part of this, whether you intended to be so or not. Will you come?"

Seth exchanged looks with Biz. She took a deep breath, "Okay."

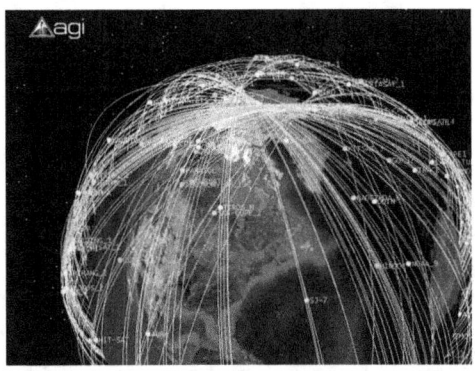

Chapter 20: Orbital

When Biz saw Terry's truck parked at the Teen Centre, she parked on the street a block away. "Let's walk." Sarah and KC passed by on their remaining 4-wheeler, the green one. It was Sarah's blue one that he had fried.

"After we've finished here, I'd like to stop by the store and pick up some fresh fruit and more munchies for the road."

Seth held his sister's hand, he didn't quite know why. She took a deep breath and walked on in.

Everyone was already there. Sarah reintroduced them, although he was sure he'd already met everyone.

"Biz, Seth. I'm glad you made it."

"Terry." She nodded, sitting next to the door with Seth rather than crossing the room.

"How are you doing, Seth? Any after effects?"

"Oh, aches and pains. I've never been zapped like that before. I'm surprised that I survived, actually."

"You wouldn't have, if you'd gotten too close to the driver coil. We were just lucky."

He cleared his throat and spoke a little louder. "Which brings me to the reason for this meeting. I think it is time to shut down and dismantle the Aurora Launcher."

There was a general murmur of disappointment among the club members. It was Bill Heath who asked, "Do we have to? Yeah, it's dangerous, but we know about that. I mean, this whole town has dangers, and we live through it."

Bill looked at Seth, "I don't mean to criticize, but you haven't grown up with this stuff like we have."

Terry interrupted. "Regardless. We had our safety rules, and they weren't enough. But that's only one reason why we should stop. I'm sure the news about the satellites has gotten around by now, but let me make it clear.

"It was one thing to experiment with a new launch technology when we were just throwing chunks of metal up into a deserted part of the sky over deserted Labrador. It's quite another to drag other people's satellites out of the sky. I've spent the whole night on the Internet searching for any stories of satellites crashing unexpectedly out of orbit, and it appears like we've been lucky so far.

"But we can't just keep doing it and hope for the best. Not now that we know the truth. As painful as it might be, we owe Seth a vote of gratitude for stopping us before we've done something really disastrous."

They were looking at Seth, and it didn't appear to him that he saw any gratitude on their faces.

Bill Heath raised his hand, like in class. "So, if the streaks weren't satellites, then there's no problem?"

Seth knew he had to say something, and now was the time.

...

"Guys, there's a lot of space junk up there in orbit. Probably what we've seen thus far is bits and pieces of broken satellites.

"Which brings up a thought that's been nagging at me since I first realized what was happening. NASA and NORAD and all the other organizations who track satellites also spend a lot of time tracking this space junk as well. It's 100% certain that they have noticed what's happened.

"It's also pretty clear that they've been hunting for what's causing it. If I were in charge, I'd have one of those spy satellites scan central Labrador, you know, the type that can read license plates on cars from orbit. Now, this is a big place, but I'm sure they've already seen your launcher. But do they understand what it is? For all they know, it's just part of the whole power distribution system.

"But if you take it down, and at the same time, the satellites stop shifting orbits, then they'd know for sure where the disturbance came from."

Everyone was listening. They were looking at each other, thinking about what was due to happen when the soldiers arrived for real.

Terry spread his hands, "When they come, it'll be for me, not for the club. I can't run away from the responsibility. But I'm open for any suggestions."

Seth realized they were all looking at him. Even Biz.

"I guess this is some kind of Tesla coil or something? Help me out here. It links up with the aurora?"

"Right. I've been building Tesla coils since high school, and I always wanted a really powerful one, with our easy access to power here. In my senior year, I made one that seemed to cause the aurora to start up every time I used it, even when there were no solar flares to fuel it like normal.

"It wasn't much, but when I was off to college, the idea that there was some link here nagged at me. I had to prove I wasn't just imagining it all. I got this job with the power company and wrangled permission on do a little research with transmission lines. Tinkering, they called it. The boss really has no idea what I've been doing, but thus far, I haven't caused any power outages and the drain I've put on the system is small enough that no one has complained."

"You mentioned a magnetic column?"

"Yes, something like that. What we've built here is the largest high frequency resonating system ever built. Nikola Tesla himself never had access the power we have here. I took the basics from Tesla's own Colorado Springs Notes, and applied it to our unique circumstances.

"I was never trying for huge lightning bolts, but rather enhancing the magnetic effects. It's a tunable coil, hooked to a modern optical system that points straight up. Research into aurora has demonstrated that there was a great deal of unorganized energy confined in the Earth's magnetic field. Energy that could be tapped by a suitable triggering signal.

"In some ways it's like a laser system. The high altitude plasma is pumped full of energy by the particles emitted from the Sun and normally it discharges randomly in the Northern and Southern Lights. It's the same way on many of the other planets with a magnetic field.

"My system had to match the natural resonance of the aurora to find the right frequency, but once the sky and the ground are in sync, the energy goes into creating this magnetic field. Energy from both ends meets in the middle. It's like a break in a dike, or a magnetic version of a huge lightning strike. The magnetic field spikes so high I've never been able to measure it.

"I had hoped to harness that magnetic spike to create a launch system, but there doesn't appear to be any way to put something into orbit. It's only straight up and down. Even though we got the cylinder probe to California, that was a fluke, and we never reached orbital velocity, even if there had been a way to point the power in the right direction." He sighed. "The idea that I was pulling stuff down at the same time just never occurred to me."

Seth nodded emphatically, "You should never abandon the launch possibilities. There's great promise there, but just for now there's another idea you should pursue! Where's a web browser? I want to show you something."

He fumbled with the search engine, but he'd seen it recently, so before too long, he found the www.fbo.gov page he was looking for.

"This is it. The DARPA Orbital Debris Removal project page. See, the US government is looking for businesses with ideas on how to clean up the tens of thousands of scraps of junk that are orbiting the Earth."

Sarah moved in and put the computer display up on the plasma TV. Everybody shifted their seating to get a better look.

"Probably, it was the 2009 collision between an Iridium phone satellite and a Cosmos Russian military communication satellite that triggered this. All of a sudden, the amount of space junk was a lot bigger."

KC asked, "So we did a good thing, pulling stuff out of orbit?"

"Yes, likely. Flying in space is getting to be as dangerous as flying low over a pond in duck season. Spacecraft are constantly getting little dings like shotgun pellets. A space shuttle had a window chipped by something small like a fleck of paint. It's getting really messy up there, and this DARPA project is looking for ideas on how to clean it up. All the time, the space station is having to make course corrections, just to avoid some little chunk of booster or ancient obsolete satellite. And you probably know as well as I do that just recently, they didn't zig as fast as they should have and had one of their solar panels damaged. They could have easily lost the crew.

"The DARPA request shows that the US government will pay real cash money for a company that comes up with a way to clean junk out of Near Earth Orbit space."

People started talking. Seth sat back and played with the search engine, pulling up YouTube videos of the 2009 collision showing the calculated debris field and others that showed just how cluttered space was getting.

Bill asked, "How much would they pay?"

Terry said, "Hold on. I've always known that I'm doing this with company equipment, with company resources. If anyone makes money on this, it will have to be the company."

If some of the faces lost smiles as visions of sports cars and fancy houses down south faded, Terry's face was showing a smile for the first time. Biz looked pleased as well.

"You'll have to go public with this. And soon."

Sarah had been reading another screen. "How will DARPA believe us? And that's a US government thing isn't it? Will they pay attention to Canadians?"

KC was looking at the computer animation of the space junk in orbit. "Some of this stuff never gets close to us."

Terry was looking at the same thing. "Yes, the orbits around the equator are unreachable, as well as any debris in high orbit, but just look how much of this stuff is in polar orbit. Just cleaning out a fraction of this will make all of the lower orbits safer, and the lower orbits are where the space station flies."

Biz asked, "What do you need to do? Make a technology demonstration?"

Sarah looked at the web page and said, "Uh, oh. They had a deadline for proposals, and we've already missed it."

Seth shook his head. "Don't mind that. You've got a game-changer here, and they won't let a little deadline get in the way of that."

She agreed. "Yes, a demo will prove to DARPA that we're not just a bunch of crackpots. We'll need something dramatic to get their attention."

Bill Heath nodded vigorously. "Demo beats a paper proposal any day! If we could say to NORAD, 'Hey look here at 12 midnight on this day' and bring some junk down, then that would be proof enough."

"I don't mean to object," Seth said, leaning back from the screen, "but a demonstration could just bring the military down on you that much faster. We are a serious threat to some very valuable hardware."

Sarah pointed to a new page on her screen. "This site has a database of satellites. If we could calculate our demo to happen when no cataloged satellites are in danger, and make that point to them, then that would go a long way to demonstrate that we're trying to be careful."

Terry nodded. "Okay, are we in agreement?"

When no one objected, he pointed to Sarah, "You're our computer expert. Calculate our safe times for demos."

"How soon?"

"The sooner the better. We could still be arrested at any moment. Nighttime, so we can show off the aurora and the space junk reentry streaks."

Seth asked her, "Did you tell Terry about our spy?"

She shook her head, and they quickly rattled off what they'd seen yesterday.

"But you haven't seen him since?"

"No."

"Okay, we can't assume he really is looking for us, but we can't ignore the possibility either. People, we're on spy-movie status. Stay clear of each other. No one should approach the launcher. Don't talk about anything in public."

Seth had been wavering, sometimes saying 'you' and then other times saying 'we'. He turned to his sister, "Biz, are we staying?"

She looked startled at the question.

Terry asked her, "I could really use your help getting the control circuits ready. I have some changes in mind that could give us much tighter control of the timing. And maybe extend the altitude."

She sighed. "Okay, I guess we could stay another couple of days, if it's all right with you, Seth?"

She looked at KC, "Can you get us a room at the Black Spruce?"

"Your same room is available. I can mark it taken."

"Okay, but I'll be working at Terry's place until we're done."

Seth asked, "But, Terry, if they put the pieces together, your house will be the first place raided. You need to work somewhere else. Especially if my sister is with you."

Bill raised his hand, timidly. "You can use my house."

"Would it be okay with your parents? What would we tell them?"

He started to turn red. "I...I already told them what's going on. They wouldn't let me go out to the launcher at night unless I told them."

"And it's okay with them?"

He nodded.

"Okay, your house it is then."

"Seth, will you come with us?"

He shook his head. He had been wondering just how secret this launcher was in truth, if Bill's parents knew. Didn't parents talk to each other?

"No. I've got to work on the official DARPA application. If it comes from me, a US citizen, then we side-step the Canadian thing, right at first. I'll work at the library, if that's okay. I'm a tourist. They won't be looking for me at all."

Chapter 21: Soldier Boy

With his sister's laptop under his arm, and Sarah's with hers, they walked over to Town Centre.

"I've never done something like this before," she confessed. "What if I do it wrong and we destroy some billion dollar satellite?"

He shrugged. "Like Terry said, he's the adult. They'll come after him." *And Biz too.* "Just do your best. Probably the expensive ones are all at a higher altitude anyway. The lower the altitude, the more they have to spend on station-keeping rockets to overcome the atmospheric drag."

He was making it up out of bits of knowledge from watching NASA TV for years, but he didn't really know for sure. There were just too many satellites from too many countries for a mere human to remember. That's why she had to use the databases. Luckily, watching satellites sail by overhead in the night sky was popular enough that there were dedicated search engines for that.

Secretly, he worried about small satellites that weren't large enough to be visible. Were the public databases good enough? But he didn't want Sarah to get freaked out by it all, so he didn't say anything.

When the glass windows of the library showed up, with all the signs and posters advertising school events and library book giveaways, he wasn't really looking inside.

But Sarah was. She grabbed his arm and pulled him back the way they came.

"What's up?"

"Our soldier boy is inside the library, using his laptop. Let's go find a seat in the restaurant."

He was ready to go find a different building altogether, but she found them a booth next to the wall where they could keep an eye out for anyone coming in. They both opened their laptops and got to work.

The idea that some soldier/spy was on the same local network as they were was unnerving. Seth took an extra minute to confirm that his firewall was up and running.

Then he got to business, downloading everything he could find from the DARPA project page. The official Request for Information had come and gone, but he'd need to fill out the same kind of document anyway, just to show that he was trying to work within the system. He started link-hopping, building a collection of names, email addresses and related sites.

He certainly didn't start filling in any forms.

It was going to be a race, giving DARPA enough time to react, while giving no hint to the military investigators already looking for them.

	Knock knock, are you there?
nickyWhy	

A private message arrived.

	Yes, and I'm going to need your help sometime soon. Do you still have your tor setup?
SethPartner	

The tor network was designed to hide people's network activities by bouncing requests all over the world. Political activists, criminals and people cheating on their spouses used it to hide their actions. Seth had never bothered with it, but Nick had bragged of using it to augment his music collection.

Sarah reached across the table and grabbed his arm. "I've got him!"

"Who? What?"

"Soldier Boy. I've got his laptop."

"What do you mean?"

She grinned. "He left his shared folder open with the default password. I've worked on this network, and I can control the routers in this building. Want to see what he's working on?"

She swiveled her laptop around and scooted around to his side of the table. Side by side they opened up the folders and took a look.

There were several with current date stamps. He clicked on an image file. It was an annotated image from space, taken last night from the International Space Station. A Russian cosmonaut had been taking pictures of the aurora last night and he posted the image to his blog. It clearly showed a glowing filament from the aurora layer down to the ground, "somewhere in Labrador" It was probably taken the same moment he was getting zapped.

"I know that blog," Seth pulled it up from his bookmarks, and there it was. A whole entry had been dedicated to the strange image, and the comments were already in the hundreds.

"It's public now. Thousands of space curious people know about this blog. It'll be all over the Internet."

With a feeling of fear, he flipped his twitter client over to the public channel. There was a message from Nick from earlier in the morning.

	@SethPartner Hey, you're in Labrador, did you see this http://bit.ly/TXqY3
nickyWhy	

He almost answered back, but Sarah stopped him. "If you say yes, he'll retweet it and thousands of people will be following you, asking about it. We're not ready for this yet."

"I can't lie to him."

"Then just ignore it for a bit. We can use the publicity later, if we've got our act together."

"What will we do about Soldier Boy? Can we get to his email?"

They searched and found his email directory, but everything was encrypted.

"I can't crack that."

Seth looked worried, "He has to be asking questions. Sooner or later, he'll ask the right person."

"Not too many secrets last long in this town. He'll question you. Tourists who stay longer than a couple of days are fodder for conversation, especially now that Dad will be griping about the fried ATV."

"I'd just better have my story straight."

They went back to work, keeping an eye out for people in the hallway.

...

KC came by with the confirmation that they had their room at the Black Spruce. "Your sister asked if you could move the pickup back to the lodge."

Seth had been fretting over his garbled paragraph–his summary for the DARPA application. It still didn't read brilliant and professional like he hoped it would. If it read like a high school homework assignment, they'd throw it out as a joke. His first had been too dumb and simple, and the second draft had used so many big words that it was even worse. "Okay, I might as well take a break from this."

Sarah glanced at her watch and closed her laptop as well. "I've got to go by the house. I'll catch up with you later." She headed for the door.

They had never seen Soldier Boy from their booth, but there were multiple ways he could have left. All they knew is that his laptop dropped off the network about thirty minutes after they first hacked it.

Seth turned to KC. "Go tell Terry that the soldier we saw Sunday is still around, and he definitely is looking for an aurora maker. But we don't know where he is right now."

His eyes got wider and he quickly looked around. "Okay, which one was he? I've pumped gas for the soldiers, what does he look like?"

"Light brown hair. Not wearing a uniform. He was in a flannel jacket. I don't know. I'm not good at descriptions. But he still looks like a soldier."

"I hope he's not looking for me."

"Just deliver the message."

And then he was alone again. Laptop under his arm, Seth trekked across town looking around and trying not to look suspicious at the same time. How long did visitors have to be here before every face was familiar? That had never been the case back in Fresno. There were too many people. But this was a different place. You could walk the whole place and memorize every street.

At the pickup, he fumbled in his pocket for the key, and then had to set the laptop on the hood while he dug around in his jacket. Finally, there was the touch of metal on a key ring and he brought it out.

The simple key brought back the pride from that day they'd gone to the store to get his own key made. His learner's permit had been still in the works and he didn't need the key to drive until later, but having the key and the trust of his sister that made it reasonable to give it to him–that had been a day to remember.

It was beat up now. He'd given it lots of use and it rode permanently in the depths of his pocket with everything from loose change to pebbles from the beach.

It won't be long before I'm fully licensed. It will be time to start nagging Biz more seriously about getting a car of my own.

In some ways, his life back in Fresno seemed farther away than the thousands of miles that they'd driven. Strangely, coming here had felt like a one way journey. *I guess time is like that. You can't go back.*

But there was work to be done. He retrieved the laptop from the hood and drove back to the lodge.

...

Biz came by the Black Spruce to change clothes. She picked up her tool kit. "I packed this away too soon."

Seth said, "I'll need all the dates and times of the previous launches documented in the application I'm writing. Can you get me that?"

Just then, in flannels and jeans, Soldier Boy walked into the entrance way with his duffel.

"Hi, California. I thought you were gone."

Seth's mind raced. *Had he heard anything? What is he doing here? Why is he talking to me?*

Then, like his mind caught in a groove and settled into a straight track, he relaxed. He would play the role of Big Bud Jackson!

"California?" he asked the soldier.

A nod and he smiled. "I saw your license tag when you were here before. I thought you'd be gone on down the highway by now."

"No," Seth grinned, his mouth making stuff up without planning, remembering how Bud Jackson always talked. "You've seen the girls here? If all the California guys knew what was hiding up here, the population would triple overnight."

Soldier Boy chuckled.

"Seth!" Biz scolded.

"Hey, don't give me that. You're chasing after a local guy yourself. Besides, Rule Six."

She blushed, and with her coat draped over her tool kit, she went to the door.

"Where are you going, Sis?"

"None of your business, Rule Six."

"What was that all about?" He set down his duffel and relaxed in a public room chair.

Act friendly.

Seth smiled at the door where she had gone. "Oh, it's a brother/sister thing."

"I wondered. She acts like your mother."

"She almost is. Legal guardian and all that. But we've got our family rules." He grinned again. "Rule Six is that we can't gripe about each other's romantic interests."

He chuckled. "I wish I'd had a rule like that when I was your age."

Seth pointed. "What's with the plaid shirt? Aren't you a soldier? Canadian Air Force or something like that."

He patted his duffel bag. "I'm on leave. The rest of the unit is off to install the upgrades in Labrador City and they don't need me to hold their hands. I've heard this place has good fishing. I'll hook back up with them when they're done."

He stretched out his hand. "I'm Jake."

"Seth." He shook it. "I've met a guy here. Younger brother of a girl I'm spending some time with. He knows about the fishing spots. He took me down to the river the other day."

"Sounds good. I've been busy, attending to the installation. But you've been all over the place. I keep seeing you with the locals. I'd be grateful if you could help me make some contacts."

He asked about California, and Seth was happy to let him in on all the high school gossip from Fresno. He was more reluctant to talk about Biz and why they found themselves in Labrador.

"It's sticky, and if my sister suspected I said anything about her former boss and why she was laid off, I'd be in serious trouble. As for me, I'd take any excuse to travel and as long as she's in a mood to stay away from home, I'm happy."

While it would be amazing if his story of going fishing proved to be the truth, Seth had no intention of believing it. Not after what he'd seen on the soldier's laptop. The big question was whether Jake was on his own, like an old-time private eye, or instead a modern spy with a radio in his ear in constant communication with his superiors. The new radio installation was a wild-card. What was that about? Was it for airplanes, or just to help the military stay in touch with each other?

The people of Churchill Falls were so used to being isolated that the idea that everyone else in the civilized world carried a personal cell phone was still a little alien to them. Their own cell service had just started recently. Phones calls were made house to house, rather than person to person.

Any story he gave Jake had to be verifiable, just in case he relayed it all to some central office that could check up on it. The photos of last night's auroras from the space station were a strong indication he was checking in with his laptop on at least a semi-regular basis.

They both stopped chatting when footsteps on the wooden floor sounded at the entrance.

Sarah walked in and then stopped in mid step as she saw Jake, the Soldier Boy himself, sitting there.

Chapter 22: Gametime

"Jake, this is Sarah." He reached out and pulled her close, just like a boyfriend might. Luckily, she didn't pull away.

"Sarah this is Jake. He's one of those soldiers we've been seeing in town. He's taken a leave to go fishing."

She nodded. "Hello."

"Since Jake is looking for a fishing guide, I was wondering if KC could take him to the river or the lake, since he's the expert."

She shook her head. "Umm. That might be a little difficult."

"Oh?" Jake asked.

She looked at Seth. "It's Dad. He's absolutely convinced that KC is the one who ... crashed the 4-wheeler. He's grounded. So, he's limited to where he can get on foot for the time being."

"Oops. It was my fault," he explained to Jake—not really explaining anything.

"I could probably give you the number of a regular fishing outfitter to call?"

She set down her laptop on the table and started searching, her back turned to them.

Seth gave her a good look and exchanged a grin with Jake. She was indeed a fine representative of Churchill Falls girls.

She gave Jake the number, then asked Seth, "Are you ready to go?"

"Let me get my laptop. Have you made contact with Moose and Clara?"

Jake asked, "Who are they?"

"Fresno friends of mine. I actually met Sarah here on the Internet. We have a gaming group. Gotta go now. There's no Wi-Fi here in the lodge."

Jake said goodbye, and they had to force themselves to walk out slowly, rather than escaping at a run.

He called after them, "Hey, if your sister comes back. Do you have any message for her?"

Seth laughed, "No. Rule Six."

...

She whispered, "Is he following us?" Her voice was unsteady.

"I can't tell. But that plain white van is probably his vehicle. We need to keep an eye out for it."

She glanced that way. "I've never seen it before."

"Looks like one of those fleet vehicles, usually painted with the company logo and advertising. It isn't one of those military trucks he came in on. Probably a rental?"

"Maybe."

When they turned the corner and had a couple of buildings in the way, she stopped and asked, "He scared me when I walked in. What happened before I got there?"

"Not much. He had been at the lodge before, and he'd mostly ignored me then. This time he was chatty."

He grinned at her, "My excuse for staying in Churchill Falls is all the pretty girls."

"Oh. That explains it. But was it wise being all friendly with him and mentioning Moose and Clara?"

"Better than sounding suspicious. Besides, having a game scheduled explained why you showed up with a laptop and why I left with mine. I figured you'd catch my drift."

"I understood. But now you realize we've got to hold hands and sit close while we can be seen in public?"

He smiled. "If I thought you'd be squeamish...."

"I'll manage. I came to give you the dates and times of the previous launches, like you asked. By the way, where are we headed?"

"We need a connection, and Town Centre would be the first place he'd look if he's trying to spy on us. How about the Teen Centre?"

"It's busy right now. We aren't the only ones who like the big screen. How about the RV?"

"Your Dad?"

"He has a late shift. It'll be okay. I use the RV sometimes when I want quiet. As long as they can see me in the window, alone, they leave me be."

They slipped into the RV without attracting attention. She took the table by the window, with the drapes open. He perched, cross-legged on the bed out of sight and logged in.

"How are the orbits coming?" he asked as he started entering the list of previous launches into his DARPA proposal document.

"I don't like it. This system is designed to list visible satellite passes, and it has a filter that ignores satellites that pass by in the middle of the night when there's no sunlight to reflect off of them. I'm extending the range by querying several other locations as well, but it's just not a comprehensive list."

The launch list showed her problem clearly. Every one of the previous tests had happened near midnight. Satellites were in sunlight most of the time, except when they passed through the shadow of the Earth, and the surface directly below was in the middle of the night.

"If the launcher will work pre-dawn or evening, then we'll just have to plan our demonstration then. It's probably not even that much of a problem. As late as your sunset is this time of year, satellites would be visible pretty late. We just have to show that we're making every effort to avoid damage to working satellites. In my proposal, I'm emphasizing that NASA or some government agency would be picking the times to clean space junk in a production system. We just have to do this one last demonstration."

She nodded and worked for a while, stretching out the kinks from time to time. He couldn't help but be aware that they were alone, private, and she could just take a couple of steps to join him on the bed.

She looked up from her screen and smiled at him. He forced his attention back to the document. *Stick to business.*

A few minutes later, he heard a distinctive sound, the clang of a sword coming from a laptop's tiny speakers. He instantly hopped onto the game server himself and avatar to avatar, they battled to a bloody finish.

"Ooh. That felt good." She vanished from the battlefield. "But back to work."

...

A twitter screen flickered open just as he closed the game window.

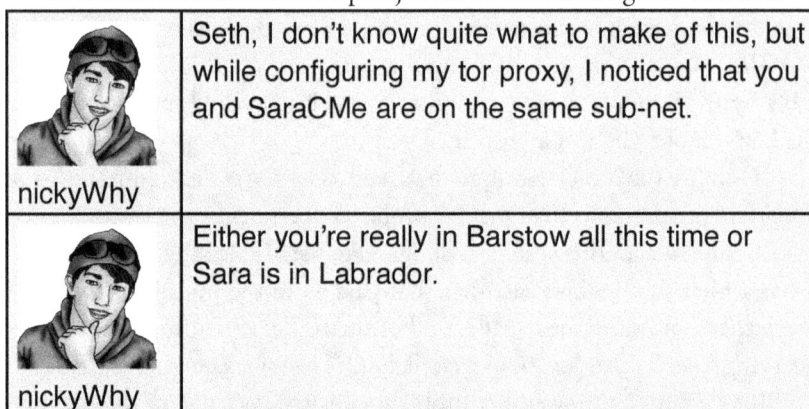

| nickyWhy | Seth, I don't know quite what to make of this, but while configuring my tor proxy, I noticed that you and SaraCMe are on the same sub-net. |
| nickyWhy | Either you're really in Barstow all this time or Sara is in Labrador. |

"Sarah, Nick has blown your cover."

"What do you mean?"

"I've just got a private message from him, outing you."

Sitting at the table, she tapped away furiously. "Seth, open your firewall for a VNC connection."

He did so with a few clicks, and as she connected with his laptop, his cursor moved away under her control and she scrolled back his message list.

"It was the game, it had to be. He was online and looked at the connection log."

Seth reclaimed his cursor and typed.

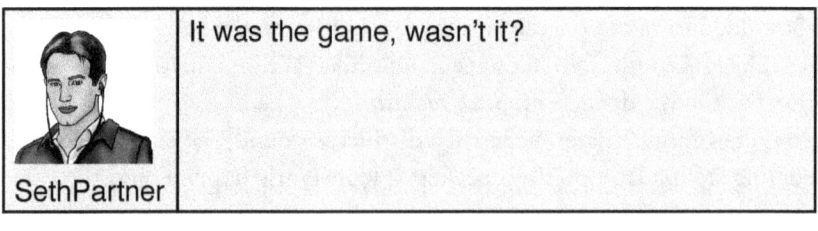

| SethPartner | It was the game, wasn't it? |

nickyWhy

Looking at Sara's tweets, I'd say Labrador.
She uses British spellings every now and then.
What's going on?

Sarah grabbed his pointer again and typed her own reply.

SethPartner

Hi, Nick. This is Sarah, hijacking Seth's laptop.
I've got him stretched out on my bed right now.

Seth struggled to regain the cursor when he realized what she was typing, but she clicked send before he could delete it.

"Cut that out. You don't know Nick! He won't keep that a secret."

nickyWhy

Hi, Sara.h. What's going on? You've got to let
me in on this. Freaky auroras, mystery spots,
unknown capsules, and now Mata Hari?

"Let me answer it, please."

He assumed it was okay to tell him, now that she'd left him no other alternative.

SethPartner

Nick. In all seriousness, we need your help, and
pls keep the gossip until l8tr. Sarah is part of a
grp here in CF that triggered aurora.

He spelled out the simple plan, and Nick's part in it all.

nickyWhy	Wow. So Sarah was spying on you from the beginning. And you're all ready to spark some kind of international incident between Canada & US.
SethPartner	That's about it. If we pull it off, all is roses. Otherwise, it get's nasty. Are you in?
nickyWhy	Of course. We'll need to bring Moose & Clara in, at least at the last minute, but sure. Wouldn't miss it.
SethPartner	Thanks. It'll really help.

"Sarah, do you want to add anything?"

"I just sent my own reply from my account. Complete with hugs and kisses."

...

There was a click and a whoosh as air spilled out the RV door.

"Sarah, what are you doing out here?"

It was George, her father. Seth stopped breathing, and ever so slowly closed his laptop lid. Standing at the door outside, Mr. Clarke was out of sight, and hopefully, so was he. Luckily, he'd never turned on the overhead light in the bedroom, so he was hidden in the darkness. He was desperate to find a better place to hide, in case the man climbed the steps and came in, but he didn't dare.

"Just talking with my Internet friends." She shifted her laptop. Whether it was to show him innocent open windows or to hide them, he couldn't see from his position.

"Well, it's getting late. You'd better come on into the house."

She sighed, and closed her laptop. Without looking his way, she turned off the lights and went down the squeaky metal steps and closed the door behind her. He was alone in the dark, and only as their footsteps retreated toward the house, did he resume breathing.

That would have been uncomfortable. He'd never have been able to talk his way out of it.

Carefully blocking the light, he reopened his laptop once he heard the sound the front door to the house closing. He adjusted the screen brightness to minimum.

He really should get out of there, but there were still things he had to finish, and he needed an Internet connection.

SaraCMe	@SethPartner Are you okay? Sorry about that.
SethPartner	@SaraCMe Fine. *practicing my ninja typing skills*
SaraCMe	@SethPartner LOL. Stay safe.

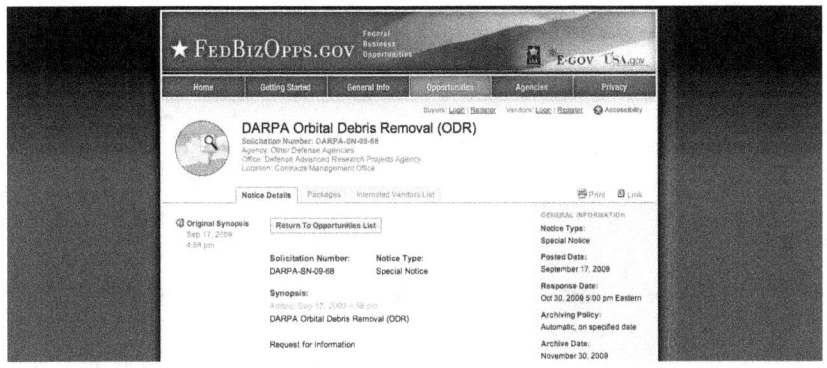

Chapter 23: Blackmail

It was near 2 AM when Seth silently crept out of the RV and walked through the chilly night air back towards the Black Spruce. The DARPA proposal was finished, except for the actual date and time of the demonstration. The last message he'd gotten from Sarah before her house lights went dark was a warning that she'd discovered a better satellite database and would need another few hours to nail down the best time.

Time is running out. But he had to trust her to solve her part of the puzzle. The demo wouldn't go over well if they brought down the wrong piece of hardware from orbit.

When he pulled off his shoes and the wooden floor creaked under his footsteps, a table lamp clicked on.

Jake was waiting. "Hey, did Daddy catch you?"

"What do you mean?"

"I saw you two sneak into the RV. How was she?"

"It wasn't like that. Nothing happened."

"That was my story when I was your age." Jake nodded and grinned. "Is that what you're going to tell your sister?"

"What?"

"I really ought to rat you out, if she's your legal guardian and all, but I won't, especially if you'd help me with a little project." He leaned forward and pointed to the chair next to him. "Have a seat."

"Project?" Seth sat down, worried.

"Yes. You know a little town like this is really something special. The people here are the only eyes in a million square kilometers. Tourists like you and me just pass through, but they live here and they see things that we'll never even know about. To them, something really amazing might seem just ordinary business as usual."

"Like the aurora."

He jumped on that. "Exactly like the aurora. Californians probably never see it in their life, but it's so commonplace up here that they don't make a big deal of it."

"What do you want me to do?" *Play it stupid. Make him spell it out. I'm just here for the girls.*

"You're making friends here, like that tasty Sarah of yours. In the time I have, I'd never make the contacts that you already have. I'm looking for something spectacular, like the aurora, that they might know about but would never mention to me."

"Why do you want to know?"

"Oh, I'm thinking of writing an article about the place, about living in this isolation. I won't be a soldier all my life. Do this little bit of research for me and your sister will never have to know what you've been up to while she was out of sight. What do you say?"

Seth nodded. The article for a travel magazine was hardly a first rate cover story, but maybe he thought it was good enough for a high school kid. It was plain that he was still fishing for the launch site, or the group that was responsible.

He's still in the dark. He had been here in town when that photo from the space station was taken, and he hadn't seen a thing. Whether the washed out sky from the street lights had hidden it, or possibly he'd just been inside or looking the wrong way. In any case, he hadn't noticed what was happening right under his nose.

Deliberately, Seth straightened himself up. "What do I get out of it? I'm on vacation here. Why should I run around doing your work for you?"

"Your sister wouldn't like the idea of her little brother getting..."

"My sister will believe what I tell her, over what some snoopy soldier says that she's only met once. And then she'd give you scolding that'd char your ears for following an under-age boy around town and spying on him."

Jake nodded, never losing his composure. "Perhaps. But then, what would Mr. Clarke say when I tell him what was happening out in his RV? You might just find that our police are a bit more protective of our young ladies than you Californians might expect."

Seth nodded, looking down at the floor. Now was not the time to declare his solidarity with the science club. That would only convince him that he was in the middle of the conspiracy and make him push harder. He needed to stay on top of what Jake the soldier boy was planning, while leading him in the wrong direction.

"I'm not sure we're going to be staying more than a day or so as it is. I'd hardly be able to find out anything in the time I've got left."

"Love 'em and leave 'em, eh?" He waved Seth off to bed. "I'll hear from you in the morning."

...

Seth was in bed when Biz came in an hour later. Jake was still up and they exchanged an innocuous greeting before she came in. Seth put his finger to his lips when she walked into the bedroom. As she closed the door, he opened the laptop and typed a message.

OFFLINE	Jake the soldier is trying to blackmail me into spying for him Saw Sarah and me sneak into RV for net. Thinks sex.

The program warned that there was no signal to send the message, but that wasn't the point.

Biz looked angry. She deleted the message and typed her own.

OFFLINE	The launcher upgrades nearly finished. Ready for Demo any time after mid-day.

They swapped again.

OFFLINE	Just waiting on the final orbital window from Sarah then. I've finished my DARPA proposal. Could you proofread it?

He handed the laptop over to her and opened the window with the document. She leaned back on her bed and read. A couple of times she made corrections, a few wording changes, and an added sentence or two.

Then, as he was almost dozing off, she tapped him on the arm. Pointing, with a frown on her face, she tapped the window of an old message.

 SethPartner	Hi, Nick. This is Sarah, hijacking Seth's laptop. I've got him stretched out on my bed right now.

Oops. He typed:

OFFLINE	Just a joke on Nick when he figured out Sarah was spying on us from the beginning. Honest.

She set the laptop aside, not replying again. He assumed she understood it was all innocent. But maybe not. He had no way of knowing what she and Terry had been up to working long hours alone. Maybe it wasn't his business. Rule Six.

It was a long night, knowing Jake could probably hear anything they said through the walls. And it was going to be a long day tomorrow.

···

Biz shook him awake. It was light, but he really wanted to sleep some more–maybe another dozen hours or so.

"He left about ten minutes ago. This might be the best time to get up." She grabbed a change of clothes and dashed over to the bathroom for a shower.

He looked out the window, searching for any sign of Jake or his white van, but he was gone. *Probably off to the library again. He's suffering from lack of connection as much as I am.*

When Biz came back out, still brushing her hair, he asked, "Where will you be today?"

"With Terry, out of sight, I hope. Can you handle the soldier? Should I turn you loose to drive 50 miles down the highway and hide out?"

He shook his head. "As long as he's playing this blackmail game, I'm okay, but it's a good idea if I run out of options. We saw some side roads near here. But I can't run yet. I need Sarah's calculated time for the demo and then I need to get the DARPA document into the right queue at the right time."

She looked at him seriously, with worry causing a shine around her eyes. "Seth, do you really think this will work? Terry's bet everything on it. He could end up in jail."

He shrugged, "I think we have a chance. If I didn't, I'd have forced you to leave with me while we still could. He isn't the only one who could end up arrested."

But it was a question that nagged at him. There were too many players in the game, and he didn't know half of them. Maybe he should have kept his mouth shut when Terry was ready to shut it all down. Maybe that wouldn't have stopped people like Jake from discovering what had happened, but they could have at least been far down the road when everything went sour.

"Well, I'm gone." She picked up her things. She sniffed the air. "You need to take a shower too, while you have the chance."

"Thanks a lot, Sis." But he'd already had that thought. He needed to put more ointment on his burns, and it did no good to stink. Better Biz griping about it than Sarah.

...

She must have been looking for him, because her 4-wheeler...or rather KC's 4-wheeler drove up before he'd walked twenty yards toward Town Centre.

Sarah gestured to the space behind her. "Soldier Boy is in the library on his laptop. Do you want to see what he's doing?" Her grin was infectious, and he hopped on behind her.

She parked around the corner from where the plain white van sat and they set up their laptops at the same booth in the restaurant.

Sarah began her infiltration into the soldier's laptop. "He can't be a trained spy. This hole in his system is elementary stuff. Do you think they just grabbed some guy at the base in Goose Bay and sent him up here to search for us?"

"I don't know. He's already made a credible attempt to blackmail me into helping in his search."

"What? What did he say?"

He leaned a little closer. "He saw us in the RV last night and assumed the worst. He threatened to tell Biz, and then when I objected, he threatened to tell your father, and maybe the police, to protect your virtue."

Sarah's face grew red, and he could see the anger in her eyes. "What did you say?"

He shrugged, "I'm just a dumb Californian, swept up in things I don't understand. I agreed to help if he kept quiet. Of course, I resisted, but now I'm supposed to 'help' him track down leads. He did seem particularly interested in auroras."

She had the same look in her eye as she had that day when he caught her wreaking havoc on that video game.

He cautioned her, "You'd better not let him get close enough to try the blackmail on you. We don't want a murder investigation added to this mess."

She ducked her eyes and nodded.

"There's a new document in Soldier Boy's directory. Let me see...."

It was an email enclosure that Jake had downloaded and decrypted, and then saved in the place where they found it.

The letter started out harsh. The first paragraph jumped right out.

"You asked for this assignment! You were in place, on the ground when the event was happening and you saw nothing??? We can't afford to waste time with your silly cloak and dagger efforts!"

The Canadian Space Agency was pressuring the Canadian Air Force to locate the orbital disturbance source, and his boss was feeling the heat. There was also a list of contact numbers that would give Lieutenant Jacob James the ability to call in troops from Goose Bay if he needed them.

While they were reading the details, the connection closed.

"He's on the move."

Sarah used copy and paste to save the contents of the document to another file, and then closed the lid.

"Come over here to this side. I'm supposed to be romancing you!" She hopped over and he had his arm around her waist when Jake walked by. He was sure he caught a flicker of the man's eyes their way.

"He saw us, I'm sure," he whispered.

Sarah giggled inappropriately and whispered in his ear, "Hey, I have to make it look like I'm stuck on you or something. We have to keep him from calling in the troops. That could stop everything. We've got the demonstration scheduled after midnight, a ten minute window when there are not supposed to be any satellites in range."

"Are you sure?"

"No! I'm sick over the idea we'd knock down some billion dollar secret spy satellite that's not in the databases and it'd be all my fault. But it's my best call."

"Okay, that's the last piece of my application document."

"When do we need to send it off to DARPA?"

"If we give the schedule too soon, Jake and his troops will be notified and they'll be ready to shut down the whole town, if that's what it takes, to keep the demo from happening. If we tell DARPA too late, they can't get NORAD's radars aimed to verify the demo."

"It sounds like we're running out of time in any case. Even if Soldier Jake fails, it sounds like the troops will be called in to search the area before too long. His boss sounded angry."

He opened his laptop and edited the proposal, adding her final information. She looked over his shoulder, still hanging on like she was his girlfriend.

"What do you think?"

She read for a moment. "I guess it's okay."

"I'll pass this over to Nick. We've already talked, late last night, and he's going to do the actual submission via his untraceable tor network. He's already got a press-release summary ready to go before then, so the people in charge will have a chance to understand what's happening and be ready for the demonstration time.

"All it takes is for him to plug this into the DARPA submission website before the demo. And then we hope they take prompt action."

Chapter 24: Runaround

Seth watched her leave before he finished. It would be nice to really have a girlfriend. Right now, the race to save their project, and avoid getting caught up in the military grinder was driving everything, but he wasn't immune to the feelings she caused when she brushed up against him or whispered in his ear.

Of course, there was the overriding problem any Labrador girl and California guy would have. *We each have our own lives to live, and I'll be gone in a day or two, with luck.* And she might not even want it to be anything more than an Internet buddy relationship. It sounded like she already had her college selected–which was more than he could say for himself. Fresno State was his most probable destination, now that the Crescent City house had been sold and Biz could afford his tuition.

Stop thinking about it. Get through today.

All that he had left to do was to send the document to Nick and confirm the time to release it.

Then, there was a shadow in the hallway. Jake was coming.

He closed the document window and opened his twitter client and a game program.

	@nickyWhy The star of Flame is hidden in the cave where you saw the battle.
SethPartner	

"Hello, California." Jake sat down across from him.

He left the laptop open. *I have nothing to hide.*

"What do you want?"

"I told you. I need you to find out what's happening here in town."

"Well, I'm doing that, if you don't scare the locals off!"

"What have you found out?"

His eyes strayed toward the laptop, where there was no sign that Nick got his rather vague message.

"Sarah heard about something. 'Something flashy', she said. We're going to meet some friends of hers at lunch that know more. She also said something about the docks, I guess on the lake, but I don't know if that's related or not."

"Okay, I'll ask around about docks. You go meet those friends of hers. See if you can get a time and location."

A new tweet arrived.

	@SethPartner Um, Seth. I'm beating at the gate, but I can't get through.
nickyWhy	

Seth pulled his laptop closer, so that the screen wasn't quite visible. "You don't sound much like a writer." He worked the keys without looking at the screen.

Jake chuckled. "Oh, I don't know. I am very good at telling stories. Don't you think Mr. Clarke would like what I have to say?"

"Shut up."

"What are you doing there?"

Seth turned the screen back where he could see it. "I'm just helping out a buddy in Fresno play a game."

Jake read the exchange. "Enough games. You'd better give me that laptop for now."

"It's my sister's!"

"She'll get it back, once our business is taken care of." He grabbed the laptop and slapped it shut. "Now get going."

...

Seth wandered over to the soccer field where a game was starting. He had dropped the firewall on the laptop, but had Nick understood what was happening? He would have had to act fast, getting his network address from the game logs like he had when he discovered Sarah was a spy, and then once the firewall was down, locate and pull the right document.

He didn't know if he would have had time to do it all, but Nick was better at that stuff than he was. He had to hope.

In any case Nick didn't know the time to send the document to DARPA.

If Jake had computer skills, he could easily tell what documents Seth had been working on in the past few days and discover everything, but somehow, the soldier didn't seem the computer geek type. He could only keep his fingers crossed.

So much had gone wrong.

"Seth!" KC walked over to him. "Sarah told me what's going on. Is the spy really looking for me? Don't let him question me. I might let something slip."

"If I can. He's still over there in the building. I'm supposed to talk to these guys. Introduce me to your friends, then get the word back to Sarah that our soldier has taken my laptop. Tell her that I don't know if Nick has gotten the document."

KC nodded. He was getting quite the workout today, running errands for everyone.

"Hey, come meet the guy from California."

None of the new people were in the Science Club, but several had heard of him.

"Are you the guy who was in Yellowstone?"

"Yeah, about ten days ago, we were dodging the Grizzly bears there."

"We've got bears here, too. Black bears."

Some of the guys weren't too impressed by the outsider and quickly returned to the game.

"Hi. I'm Ashley. Did you see the geysers?"

He nodded. "And the mud pots." He did his best to describe the smelly hot water features they'd stopped at, and told the stories about the bear jams and the buffalo jams. Of course, they'd all seen pictures and the nature TV shows about the park, but he tried to describe the odd quirks, like the damage the buffalos caused by shredding the bark off the trees and the crazy tourists who tried to chase the dangerous animals.

By lunch time, he'd keyed the Facebook names of several girls into his phone.

"Come eat with us, there's plenty."

"Great. Got a pen? I need to write something down."

Jake had appeared when he hadn't been looking and hovered around the edge of the field. He looked a little out of place since there were no other adults watching the game. Seth scribbled on a paper cup: "They're asking me to stay another couple of days so I can see 'it'." Glancing at Jake, he set the cup down and walked away with the girls.

...

They entered one of the identical houses, and still another girl was waiting there. "Here, I've got a message for you from Sarah."

There was a round of giggling and they watched as he read the note. He realized that his friendship with Sarah must have been the source of considerable gossip over the past couple of days.

"Keep SB from using phone as long as possible and bring him to demo."

'SB' must mean Soldier Boy. Okay, but why bring him to the demo?

Could that be from Terry? A plan was underway and although he wasn't in on it, he had to do his part. It was a complex game and he was in the dark. Typical. But how could he keep Jake from using a phone?

The gossip was that cell phone service had just started in Churchill Falls. Not that the service was compatible with his phone. But Jake was an outsider and might just have a phone on him. He'd have to be on a lookout. And that meant he had to stay close to Jake. Not fun.

Ashley asked, "What's that man up to?"

So they'd been watching.

"How much do you know about the science club?"

She curled her nose up. "Tesla coils and rocket ships. Geek stuff. They were all excited about something a few weeks ago, but that was right after the end of second semester and most of us were busy with other stuff."

"Well, it turns out it was something important, and that guy is some kind of spy sent to investigate. He's trying to get me find out who's acting suspicious and find out what they know."

Ashley looked like he'd just announced a party.

"He's looking for suspicious acting students?"

"Right."

She got an evil grin on her face and said, "Let me call my boyfriend. We'll give him suspicious!"

...

A guy roared up on an 4-wheeler. Ashley ran out and hopped on. They roared off towards the highway.

Seth came out of the house a few seconds later and saw Jake waiting across the road. He waved at him.

"Ashley got a call. She was excited. She and her boyfriend were going to go see something."

"What?"

"I asked, but they said it wasn't for outsiders."

Jake frowned and said, "Let's go. Come on." They ran over to the parking lot and he waved to the other side of the white van.

"Get in."

Seth looked around inside, but it was nearly bare except for the seats and a backpack. It had a new smell to it.

"Did they say were they were going?"

"Toward the lake, I think. Someone said something about dikes."

"Dikes, not docks? Was that what you heard earlier?"

"I don't know! I don't know what you're looking for. I'm just repeating what I heard."

Jake growled and concentrated on his driving.

When they got to the highway, there was some dust in the distance towards the west.

Jake spun his wheels cutting the corner and accelerating too fast for the road, heading past the power plant. A couple of miles later, there was a branch off to the north, with more dust hanging in the air.

The road wasn't paved and he had to slow down, but he kept up an uncomfortable pace. Seth snugged his seat belt tighter, and glanced at Jake from time to time. If he had a gun, it didn't show. Nor could he see a phone, but that didn't mean anything. His phone wasn't visible either.

There were signs of the massive lake off to the left and occasionally, there was dust ahead of them, but they never saw Ashley and her boy friend.

They kept on the road for twenty miles or so, until Jake turned to him. "I don't like being set up. Now tell me, where are they going?"

"I don't know. I'm from California. I didn't even know this road existed. Maybe we should go back. My sister will be wondering where I am."

He snarled and then pulled out a radio from his jacket pocket.

"Is that a cell phone?"

"No. What makes you think a cell phone would work out here in the middle of nowhere." It looked square and utilitarian, much more like a military radio than a consumer gadget. Was the new antenna at the airport supposed to work with it, or was the construction project unrelated? In any case, this was his link to his superiors.

How can I stop him from using it? Jake was ten years older and with the muscles of a trained soldier. There wasn't even a wrench or tire-iron to use as a weapon, even if he could bring himself to try.

Jake snarled and got out of the van and raised the radio high, trying to get a signal, but there was no luck.

Seth looked at the steering column, where the keys should have dangled in he'd been lucky. No go. Jake had been ahead of him.

The soldier peered off at the horizon, looking for any trace of a dust cloud. He was clearly tempted to follow the road, but it seemed to stretch on forever. Was it just a maintenance road to service the dikes that kept the huge lake in its bounds, or did it go on for hundreds of kilometers to some obscure Inuit village? He didn't know. Like he'd told Jake, he was from California.

Jake was asking himself the same questions, probably.

"If I find that you set me up...." He got back in and turned the van around, facing another twenty miles of dust.

Oh well. So much for reverse psychology. His attempt to urge Jake on by pretending that he wanted to go back had failed. Seth glanced at his cell phone. There was no signal for him either, but he was really interested in the clock. If he had only gone another hour up the road! But sunset wasn't coming soon enough.

What if I could let air out of a tire, like KC had tried on me? But that idea came too late.

As they approached Churchill Falls, Jake stopped the van and again tried to use his radio, and was frustrated by his inability to get signal. "The middle of nowhere," he muttered. Seth unbuckled and opened his door.

"You get back inside. Stay put. Don't do a thing unless I tell you to."

They drove back to Town Centre.

"Stick with me." Jake pulled his laptop from his backpack and stalked towards the restaurant.

He snarled at the waitress when she tried to get an order from him. "Fries and gravy," Seth ordered. Jake opened his laptop and tried to get on the local Wi-Fi.

It seemed like he was having a lot of trouble. Jake was getting a signal, but every time he made a connection and started to activate his email, the signal would drop.

Seth's fries arrived and he munched on them. He suspected that Sarah was around somewhere in some equipment closet having the time of her life sabotaging his efforts to contact his superiors. He forced that thought away. It wouldn't help a thing if Jake saw him smile.

He ached to pull out his phone and send a few messages; one to Nick to confirm that he had the document, and another to Sarah to get an update on what was happening, but he couldn't. Not with Jake watching his every move.

Carefully, he took a napkin and in his lap, just out of sight, he scribbled, "No phone. Trying to use a walkie talkie." Maybe he could at least keep them updated.

But how to get this message to them? He looked around the room, but he saw no one from the club.

Maybe they're watching me.

He folded the napkin carefully and waited for an opportunity. He'd drop it and wait for someone to pick it up.

Jake closed his laptop. "We're going."

"I haven't paid for my fries."

He slapped a twenty on the table. "Come on."

Seth got up, carefully holding the napkin in his hand.

But Jake was observant. "What's that?"

He grabbed his hand and pulled out the note.

"So you're working with them. I thought that might be the case. Why are you interested in whether I'm using a phone?" He crumpled the note and jammed it in the gravy.

"Come with me" With a hand on Seth's shoulder and a no-nonsense grip, he steered Seth back towards the van. "I've waited long enough. It's plain that you're part of this conspiracy. And that's all I need. You're my proof.

"Sit down here, against the side." Seth leaned against the metal ribs of the inside of the van while his captor pulled nylon cable ties from his backpack and handcuffed him to the seat.

"You cause me trouble, and you'll regret it." He went back inside, probably to make a phone call.

That does it. He's calling in the troops. Struggling with his hands tied, he fished his phone from his pocket and tried to get a Wi-Fi signal. It was there, but faded in and out. Typing was hard, but possible.

	@SaraCMe I am tied up in the back of SB's van. He's heading into Town Centre to make a phone call.
SethPartner	

He'd barely pressed send and was watching an endless progress bar when there was a knock on the side of the van.

I blew it. He was stymied for lack of evidence, and I handed it to him. Regret settled down on him like heavy shackles.

It was KC, "Seth, are you okay?"

"Yes, he's got me tied up. He's inside making a phone call to his commander probably."

KC struggled with the door. "It's locked."

"Go tell Terry."

"I'll try, but he's been called to the plant. Some kind of emergency."

Seth sagged as KC left. The word was out, and Terry's bosses had been called in. Everything was lost. He saw that his tweet had been sent. Useless, like everything else.

Jake arrived, looking a lot more pleased that before. "It's over. The Canadian Space Agency got definitive word that the electro-whosits thing is based here in Churchill Falls. You tell me where it's located and I'll get it secured. Whatever your friends were planning, it's not going to happen now."

Seth tried to put the puzzle pieces together. Could Nick have jumped the gun and put the details out on the public Internet too soon? It was possible. He'd flubbed the final instructions, there in the restaurant and Nick had to wing it.

"It's just as well. I'll take you there."

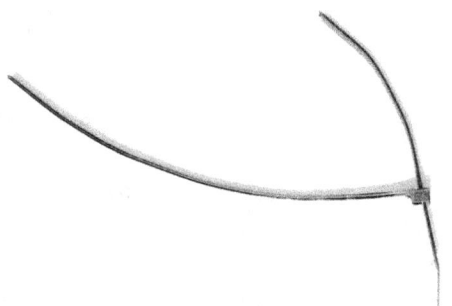

Chapter 25: Demo Time

"Get these things off me. They hurt." Jake looked skeptical.

"I know where the Aurora Launcher is," Seth insisted. "I can take you there if you'd just let me."

Jake pulled a knife with clippers from his pocket and snipped off the cable ties. Seth sat in the passenger seat. "Go to the highway and turn left."

Seth weighed the possibilities, none of them were good. If troops came in tonight and arrested them all, what would that mean for Biz? They were all active participants in the conspiracy, but most were minors. Only Terry and Biz were adults. Terry told her his superiors looked the other way at his experiments, but if there were criminal charges, they would need a scapegoat to deflect the blame from themselves.

But as for the Palmers, the best he could hope for would be for the both of them to be thrown out of the country. At worst, Biz would go to jail and he'd be turned over to some institution.

Sarah and KC probably wouldn't get off lightly, even if they did avoid the worst of it.

His gang back in Fresno were probably safe. It was an Internet lark, and they had nothing to do with the actual aurora gadget.

Jake looked his way, and Seth took his bearings. The airport passed to his right. Parked beside the largest hangar was a little green vehicle. Was that Sarah's 4-wheeler? *What's she doing there?*

"Go on as far as the bridge."

When they neared the span over the empty gorge that had contained the Churchill Falls, he gestured for Jake to pull over. They both got out.

"Where is it?"

"Give me time. I was driven here in the dark the first time I saw it. I need to get my bearings."

The sky was getting darker. "Do you know why my sister and I went for a drive all the way across the continent? It was because we didn't really have a home to go back to."

Jake was impatient, but he wanted Seth to talk, so he let him ramble. A cooperative snitch was his quickest route to success.

A noise in the sky brought both heads up, staring at the plane on landing approach.

"Is that your guys?"

"No. They're coming by helicopter."

Seth nodded. He'd wondered if Jake had actually called in his help or not. This confirmed it. How much time would it take between his call and their arrival?

"Our parents are dead, you know. When Dad came home in a box from Iraq, Mom tried to keep everything together, but it may have been the stress that kept her from holding up under the leukemia. Now my sister is trying to do the same thing."

Staring at the bare rock below, which once must have held the magnificent swirl of the lake's outflow, it felt a lot like his history. How long ago had it been, when he was just a happy kid with both parents, a big sister, and wonderful place to go visit in the summer when Fresno got too hot?

Piece by piece, that wonderful life had dried up.

There was a trickle of water still flowing in the middle of the former falls.

If that was the last chance for Biz to have a good life, then he had to take it, even if they came down on him for tricking Jake.

He saw a footpath that led from the road, probably to some scenic spot in the gorge. Jake was watching, but he wasn't in position to stop him as he suddenly made a dash down the slope.

"Hey! Stop!"

The light was poor, but Seth was down onto the scoured rock face of the gorge in seconds. He didn't look back. He could hear the soldier following. This surface was uneven, and a bit too steep for his comfort. But anything he could do to stall the troops meant more time for Biz and Terry to pull off their demo. It was the only thing that could save them all.

"Stop! You can't get away from me!"

Seth glanced back and Jake was close, too close.

That moment of inattention was a mistake. His foot slipped on a wet patch as he got too close to the stream. He went down, and the steep grade kept him rolling.

He was out of control approaching the edge, where Churchill Falls spilled down a steep cliff face into the deeper gorge below.

"Gotcha!" A strong hand gripped his foot. His tumble slowed, even as it brought Jake to the ground as well.

The water spilled over the edge just a couple of feet away. A misty breeze coming up from below caught him in the face and he gasped.

"To your feet." Jake had his arm in a hold, and practically lifted him up. Pressure on that arm kept him moving right where the soldier directed.

Seth shuddered. "I think you saved my life."

"Hmm."

At they struggled up the pathway back to the van, lighting the roadway with its headlights, Seth muttered, "I'll show you where the launcher is."

"You said that before."

"I mean it this time."

Jake put him in the passenger seat and once again applied the nylon straps.

"Go back towards town. Slow down when you pass the airport."

He didn't look very confident, but he started the van.

The dashboard lit up. Seth nodded at the clock.

"Wow, up here in the summer, sunset is really late. It's already after midnight."

Jake grumbled, but he turned the van around and headed back.

The plane Seth had seen before was parked at the hangar, but no one was on the ground. The 4-wheeler was missing too. He crossed his fingers.

A moment later he said, "Slow down here."

"Where?"

"Here it is."

Jake looked suspiciously at the rough dirt trail, but steered the van into the ruts. Fresh tread marks were plainly visible.

He scrapped the bottom a couple of times, and the wheels spun as they crossed the creek, but he did know his business as he gunned his way up the slope. Jake was showing a feral grin. He'd seen the tracks as well and sensed that he was finally approaching his target.

When Seth saw a 4-wheeler and a pickup parked ahead, he said. "Stop here. You have to kill your head lights."

"Why?"

"They have signals, and looks like someone is here already." He saw the fence line that had zapped him the other time, but it wasn't lit. *I hope I'm not too early.*

"I mean it. Stop here or we'll be fried. They've got a gazillion volts going through these wires."

Jake looked at him cautiously and then parked next to the pickup.

As soon as the van's engine went silent, a voice called out.

"There you are Lieutenant James! I was hoping you could make it in time." A white-haired man in a business suit stepped out of the darkness. He held a flashlight.

Terry and Biz stepped into the circle of light with him.

Biz saw Seth in the dome light of the van and visibly relaxed. He held up his bound hands where she could see them. She frowned and reached into her coat pocket.

"What's going on here?" Jake got out of the van.

Biz moved towards the van. Jake reached out and roughly grabbed her arm. "You stay back!" She struggled to get free, fear and anger highlighted on her face in the flashlight glare.

Seth strained at the restraining straps, ready to do battle for his sister–if he could just get free!

But Terry was there in a flash. He slapped the soldier's hand free of her arm.

"Get your hands off her!"

Biz moved past the angry faces, giving them a wide berth.

Seth watched the confrontation, feeling at one with Terry. But while he would have liked to hurt Jake right then, Terry was in his face.

Yes. He's the one.

Terry growled, "Back off! This is a space junk cleanup."

Biz reached into the van and snipped Seth's cable ties with her clippers. He was happy to get free while the soldier had his back turned.

"Not tonight, it isn't." Jake held his ground, face to face, snarl against snarl.

"And why not," asked the old man gently. Both turned to face him.

Jake answered, "Because I was ordered to stop it."

The man smiled and shook his head, looking over Jake's civilian attire.

"Well, this is crown property under the company's administrative authority, my authority, and I don't take orders from random strangers passing through."

"You know who I am. You called my name."

"Did I? I must be getting old. I don't recall that. You'll have to get me someone from the government before I can take your order seriously."

Jake pulled out his radio, but the buttons brought no response. He shook it in frustration.

Seth heard a soft chuckle from his sister. She looked at him with a grin and he knew instantly what she had done. If anyone could whip up a radio jammer on short notice, it was her. She moved quickly back to Terry's side.

Rubbing his wrists as he got out of the van, he called out to his former captor, "Don't bother, Jake. You're not going to be able to stop this and you can't keep it quiet either. While I was spinning my sad orphan-boy story, a network of people all over the world began reporting on this demonstration. If you could get your radio to work, I bet you'd find out that your superiors now know more about this event than you do. The story of the Churchill Falls Aurora Launcher and its demonstration for the Defense Advanced Research Projects Agency has already spread far and wide."

Off in the distance, there was the distinctive thrum of helicopter blades. Jake turned and off in the distance, there were the landing lights of the approaching craft.

"We'll see about that!" He pressed the radio switch, but again, the advanced digital radio couldn't sync up with the new relay tower at the airstrip.

"What is wrong with this thing?"

The helicopter lights moved behind the nearby hill.

"No!" Jake ran back along the trail, trying his radio furiously. From the sound, the helicopter had begun its landing two miles off to the northwest at the airport.

Terry was looking at his wristwatch and said, "I think it's time for the demo." He blinked his flashlight over to the control hut across the clearing and KC, barely visible from his flashlight, activated the system. The fence began glowing.

Jake came running back, "Don't!"

Seth didn't even think about it. He dashed to cut Jake off. He made a running tackle. Moose would have been proud.

They tumbled together on the ground, only this time the soil was a lot softer than the rocky gorge. "Don't go into the discharge zone or you'll be struck by lightning. Believe me, I know." Something about his eyes convinced Jake and he stopped struggling.

Sarah was at a tripod taking pictures of everything with a small camera. Jake struggled to his feet.

"You don't know what you're doing!"

The aurora started forming high overhead. The old man's eyes were on the spectacle in the sky, but he said. "Oh, I think I do. And when I report to the Premier in St. John's that the company will be able to report income from the United States government of several millions of dollars a year, totally independent of the pittance we get from giving our electricity to Québec, I think that will make a number of people pleased, don't you?"

Seth watched in amazement as the magnetic column formed from the circular fence and a glow of plasma flashed into being, stretching from the ground all the way to the heavens above. It was something he had missed the other time, being zapped by the discharge. Even at this distance, he could feel the keyring in his pocket tugging toward the shimmering light.

High above, where the column touched the glowing green curtains of the aurora above, there was a flash of a meteor, and then several more.

Seth could have watched it forever, but Terry blinked his flashlight twice across the field. The fence glow died, and the column of light vanished. One last meteor flashed, but the aurora continued to play across the sky like it had done throughout all of human history.

Terry and Biz were watching, arm in arm, and the company man nodded in approval.

Seth walked over to Sarah, where she was panning the camera back down to the ground to show the fence line now dark and invisible.

"It's done," he said.

She nodded. "At least the demo. Terry is going to have a lot of work to do. You can bet the adults will move in now and our science club will go back to watching from a distance."

"I was never so glad to see that old man here."

"Shh! Don't let him hear you call him that. He's in charge."

"Terry's boss?"

"Nearly everyone's boss. When your press release started to hit the net and he caught wind of it, he called the local office here and Terry came running. It's just good luck that he understood the potential of the launcher. He flew in from Goose Bay just a little while ago and I drove him over on the four-wheeler. You should have seen him try to keep his fancy shoes dry when we crossed the creek!"

"I wondered if Nick had gotten the message out in time."

She shrugged. "Maybe he jumped the gun a little, but it all worked out. You're going to have to get back on Twitter as soon as you can, because Moose and Clara are frantic that you've been arrested and tortured by Evil Canadian Spies."

The thrum of helicopter blades was increasing, and glowing lights appeared from around the hilltop.

"Uh, oh. They're coming to check out the strange lights."

Sarah whispered, "Quick, go pull the jammer from off the rear bumper of the van. Soldier Boy needs to be able to talk to the helicopters before they come in and damage the launcher or fly into the power lines."

He ran back to the van, and there it was, covered in mud—a small box with a little antennae, magnetically clipped to the van. He pulled it free, and felt around until he found the opening. There was a power switch.

Jake was yelling into his radio, as it suddenly started to work for him. Seth walked the slimy box over to the trees and stuffed it down out of sight. It would be best if the jammer were never discovered.

The helicopter's bright landing lights were blinding. He hurried over to be with the rest of them. Sarah handed him a camera memory card.

"Hide this in case things get out of hand."

It was probably her video. She had replaced it with another card and was filming the helicopter and the chaos as soldiers dropped to the ground.

Terry and the official were gesturing wildly, warning Jake of the danger of the 230 kilovolt power lines just beyond the landing lights. One bad move could turn this into a catastrophe.

Seth felt strangely isolated from it all. The deed was done. Everything was out of his hands now. He was just an observer.

What he could see in the bright lights were Biz and Terry, holding hands like they would never let go.

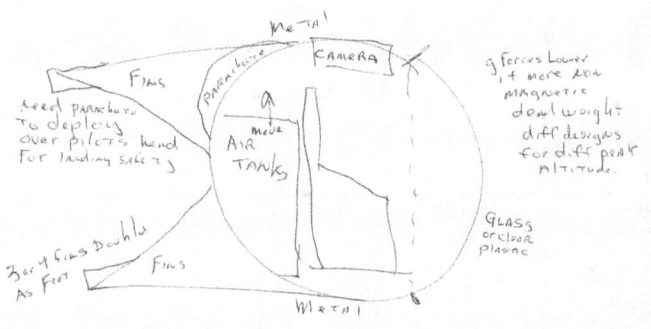

Chapter 26: New Course

So much of his past few days had been spent at Town Centre, so it was comfortable to plop down in a chair with his rescued laptop and watch the power struggles going on between the company and Jake's soldiers.

Jake had failed to stop the demo, and there wasn't much he could do at this point other than make threats.

Seth uploaded the video and started the process of moving it to YouTube.

...

 ClaraN1	@SethPartner You scum! Why didn't you tell us about this from the beginning. Do you know how much we worried about you?
moosenine	@SethPartner Yeah, bro. You know I've got my !Parents! asking about you. Not cool bein on the outside.

SethPartner	Hey guys, I'm sorry, but ya get caught up in something that u have to promise to keep secret. I didn't want to leave you out, but hey.
ClaraN1	@SethPartner So, you and Sara?
SethPartner	@claraN1 No telling. She cool. Smart and nice arm-candy.
SaraCMe	@SethPartner Hey! I'm watching you.

He looked across the room. Yes, she was working away on her own laptop. They locked eyes. Clara's question was a valid one, but considering it wasn't settled whether they would be arrested or not, maybe it wasn't the right time for a definitive answer. He could see the same worry in her eyes.

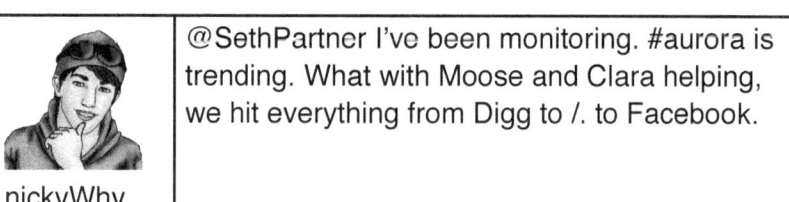

nickyWhy	@SethPartner I've been monitoring. #aurora is trending. What with Moose and Clara helping, we hit everything from Digg to /. to Facebook.

 nickyWhy	@SethPartner @SaraCMe @moosenine @ClaraN1 U should all check follow counts. We're not this private little club anymore. People are watching

Across the room, Sarah looked up with her hand on her mouth. She brushed her hair back and typed.

 SaraCMe	Oops. Hello world from Churchill Falls.

The YouTube submission was done. Seth posted an alert with its URL, complete with the #aurora hash tag. If Nick was right, soon the whole world would be watching the glowing magnetic column from Labrador.

When he looked back up, Biz was waving at him. He set the laptop down and walked over. He knew what was coming, and what he had to do.

"Hi Biz. Are they going to arrest us?"

She shook her head. "No. I think we're past that. But they're asking...."

He nodded. "You want to stay on. Maybe be Mrs. Terry?"

She glanced around to see if anyone heard. Her face was red. "Well, maybe."

"It's fine. I've already been thinking about it. Churchill Falls is a great place, and it's not long before I'd be leaving for college in any case. I was never going to stay in Fresno."

"Your friends?"

"I have friends here, friends there. We play on the Internet. Not much will change, other than I won't be watching Moose play football live. Besides, I've never gotten that picture of a moose for him. Can't leave until I've done that."

"Ok." She smiled, and nodded, unable to say much more than that.

The administrator walked up and asked, "You and your sister are here as tourists?"

Seth nodded, "At least that's how we started. My sister here would like to stay on and help with the new electronics she and Terry have been developing. I put together the DARPA proposal and I would dearly love to stay and do what I can to help. This system has so much potential!"

"That's wonderful. Well, we will have to appeal for expedited worker's visas and get you fixed with housing. Having you as part of this process will certainly make the negotiations with your government go a lot smoother." He shook hands. "I'm happy to have you as part of our little town."

Sarah had been hovering, listening. She ran up and hugged him. "This is great. Now I've got to find a way to let Dad know you're not leaving."

Seth chuckled, "He'll know already. Small town, remember?"

Biz said, "I don't know where to start. There's so much to do. We'll have to arrange a quick flight back to Fresno to handle the house there, and ...."

"Biz. Stop. Aunt Ally will be in no hurry to move. You don't need to handle everything tonight. Rule Four, we'll handle this together."

Terry looked over from his conversation with the administrator across the room. He was worried about her.

She caught his look and smiled back at him. "I guess I've been worrying about how things might change."

He laughed. "So they change. Life always changes. None of that matters except Rule One—we'll always be brother and sister. That's the only rule that counts."

THE END

Want to read more about space debris? Start here:
http://en.wikipedia.org/wiki/Space_debris

Want to read more about the Aurora? Start here:
http://en.wikipedia.org/wiki/Aurora_(astronomy)
http://www.gedds.alaska.edu/auroraforecast/

Want to read about Churchill Falls?
http://en.wikipedia.org/wiki/Churchill_Falls
http://www.ieee.ca/millennium/churchill/cf_home.html

From Crescent City, California ...

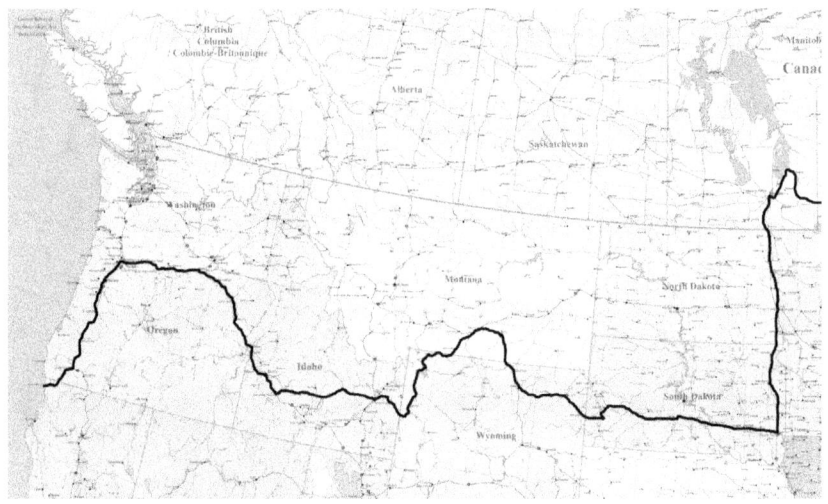

... to Churchill Falls, Labrador

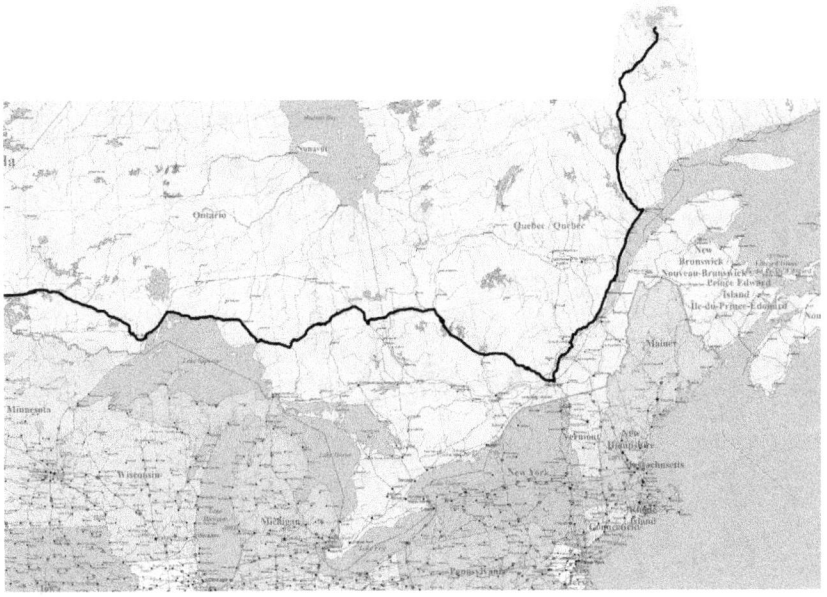

Small Towns, Big Ideas

Many titles, and more are coming. This series that appeals to age 12 and up by Henry Melton is available now. Starting in the here and now, these tales follow the trials of high school aged heros that take that extra step into the fantastic when something unexpected drops into their lives. Many of the classic science fiction ideas like teleportation, alien contact and time travel are explored in a way totally accessible to many readers who "don't read that kind of stuff" as well as being an exciting adventure for those who do. Available as paper and e-books on-line everywhere.

Henry Melton is often on the road with his wife Mary Ann, a nature photographer. From the Redwood forests to Death Valley to the Great Lakes to Delaware swamps to the African bush, scenes out the windshield become locales for his fiction work. He is frequently captivated by the places he visits, and that has inspired his latest series of novels; Small Towns, Big Ideas. Check his website, HenryMelton. com for current location, his stories, a blog of his activities, and scheduled appearances. Henry's short fiction has been published in many magazines and anthologies, most frequently in Analog. Catacomb, published in Dragon magazine, is considered a classic

Falling Bakward

by Henry Melton

ISBN 978-0-9802253-6-5

Jerry Ingram wanted to be special, more than just a sixth-generation farmer in South Dakota and spent hours after school digging at the mystery spot in the back fields, searching for Indian artifacts. With Sheriff Musgrave always picking on his family and Dad always worried about money, an important discovery would be a great lift. But those bones he found weren't Indian, and when a cave-in drove him into the metal craft buried since the last ice age he found a portal to the world of the Bak, and discovered that the gentle, zebra-striped giants had been waiting for his family for thousands of years!

❧

"...just about everyone in Jerry's family has secrets...the story flows well and is easy to follow. The Bak are an engaging race, and the Kree are suitably terrifying. I can almost see this as a '50s monster movie, but with much better characterization. Lots of thrills, plenty of suspense, and widescreen action... If you're looking for YA science fiction in the sense-of-wonder vein, check out Falling Bakward." Bill Crider, author of the Sheriff Dan Rhodes series, among many other things. 3/15/09

"His writing style is much like that of Robert A. Heinlein and Isaac Asimov when they were writing what was known at the time as Juvenile Fiction...a satisfying read for adults as well... It was quite awhile before I put it down again and then only reluctantly." Elizabeth J. Baldwin, author of Horses 3/10/09

Lighter Than Air

by Henry Melton

ISBN 978-0-9802253-1-0

**Winner of the 2009 Eleanor Cameron /
Golden Duck Award**

It could be the best prank in the history of Munising High School's unofficial Prank Day. Working for a next door neighbor inventor had left Jon Kish with unlimited quantities of lighter-than-air foam, perfect for building...say, a full-sized flying saucer! High school honor demanded it. Plus with the family stress of his mother's surgery, he needed something to keep his mind occupied. But little sister Cherry had her own schemes in play, and events more serious than high school pranks or Mother's cancer were about to focus the world's attention on this little northern town.

∽

"Lighter Than Air is a good read for the whole family that teenagers will love from start to finish! Ample scientific facts are scattered throughout the story, thus enriching the plot and feeding the mind. It is entertaining and exciting to read" Liana Metal, Midwest Book Review 12/2008

"Melton weaves a tale of secrets and suspense, science and pranks, emotion and intrigue...the tedium of the scientific jargon is minimalized by Melton's exquisite ability to tell a story...the scene where Jon and his friend and co-conspirator, Larry, unleash their UFO on an unsuspecting Halloween Festival crowd is priceless. The scary part of the story, though, is not how the characters deal with the issue of death, but that of Internet predators...I found the possibility all too real, and you might as well." Benjamin Potter, October 13, 2008

Extreme Makeover

by Henry Melton

ISBN 978-0-9802253-2-7

Lightning brought a towering redwood crashing down around her, and something dripped on her skin. After that, high school senior Deena Brooke struggled to make sense of the impossible changes to her body. She was grateful for the interest Luther Jennings had in her puzzling insights and quirky urges, until she discovered that he was hiding a deadly secret of his own. Alien nanobots had invaded her body, an unseen influence that was changing her into something else! And was Luther helping her or dragging her into some criminal scam of his own?

&

"I've recently read the #1 best-selling YA novel, and Henry's is much better written. It's also better paced and has a better story and better-realized characters. Trust me." Bill Crider, Author of the Sheriff Dan Rhodes series and others. 10/08/08

"The plot is quite tight and believable, and so are the characters. They are 'real' kids with their own family problems who try to solve the riddle of Deena's sudden change. It is a very exciting story from the very first page to the last one." Liana Metal, Midwest Book Review September 2008

"Once in awhile you read something that is really fun. If you pick up a Henry Melton book that's what you'll find...this is a superb example of young adult science fiction." Benjamin Potter, August 11, 2008

Roswell or Bust

by Henry Melton

ISBN 978-0-9802253-0-3

Teenager Joe Ferris was raised to help guests -- he was third generation in his family's motel business -- but once he connected with mute Judith, they were off on an epic thousand mile road trip through the Southwest, all to help the most unique guests of all -- the Roswell aliens stranded far from home since 1947. With the Men in Black hot on their trail, and discovering that the aliens had more tricks up their sleeves than their captors had ever discovered, Joe and Judith have to wonder just who is taking whom on the ride of their lives!

ຕ

"Reading Roswell or Bust will give let you enjoy Science Fiction, even if you haven't been a big fan in the past, and will clue you into why Melton was chosen for an award from the SF community in his first outing as a novelist. It's a great escape (and not only for the aliens who've been kept captive for many decades) Benjamin Potter, April 7, 2008

"The plot is tight... A strange talkie, a mysterious courier and a couple of spies are all involved in this exciting story that will entertain kids of that age... It caters to all the family." Liana Metal, Midwest Book Review July 2008

"...whimsically amusing. The story inside is a wonderful read...His characters are real, complete with the small concerns and everyday trials... adventures are zany and compelling, keeping the reader enthralled to the end when the book can be closed with satisfaction." Ethan Rose, coauthor of Rowan of the Wood

Emperor Dad

by Henry Melton

ISBN 978-0-9802253-4-1

Winner of the 2008 Darrell Award for Best Novel.

His dad was up to something, but it wasn't until James Hill saw the theft of the British Crown Jewels live on CNN and the bizarre claims of this new Emperor of the Earth, did he realize Dad might have invented teleportation in the shed in the back yard. Bob Hill had a plan to protect the world from his disruptive invention, but when the police forces of the world move in on him, no one knew James had hacked the family computer and had taken the power of teleportation himself. Now only he could save his family, and the world.

❧

"It follows in the best tradition of other juvenile SF/action adventure novels in that it follows a young man trying to solve the usual problems that confront any young man (the search for self-identity, relationships with girls, family, and society) at the same time as he must solve the larger problems that surround him (such as whether his father is a mysterious shadowy figure branded as a global terrorist, and what to do when FBI agents show up at the door)... great job of balancing suspense and humor...no real belly laughs, but there were quite a lot of chuckles." Chris Meadows, Teleread January 7th, 2009

"It's a fast-moving SF adventure that's a lot of fun ... Cool cover." Bill Crider -- August 1, 2007

"I had a blast reading this book! With every page turned, you don't want it to end." J. Stock August 16, 2007

Golden Girl

by Henry Melton

ISBN 978-0-9802253-5-8

Debra Barr was barely out of bed when she found herself thrust into a pivotal role in the future of the human race. Plucked out of her bedroom in small town Oquawka, Illinois to a future Earth destroyed and poisoned by a major asteroid impact, the future scientists explained how she could walk a few steps differently, and with YouTube, save the planet. But everything they told her was wrong. Instead of returning to her bedroom, she appeared two hundred years in the past, in the wilderness on the banks of the Mississippi River and it was up to her to discover the rules of time travel without killing herself or anyone else in the process. Bouncing through time, only one thing was certain, anything she decided to do could mean life or death for her family and friends and the route she chose would likely cost her everything. Unfortunately, the more she discovered, the more she suspected that everyone was lying to her.

స్

Not Your Usual Time Travel Story

"Stories that give serious consideration to the issues of paradox and causality in time travel are few and far between. But Henry Melton's latest young-adult book, Golden Girl, is one that treats time travel the right way. It starts from an interesting premise, adds a unique time travel mechanic, and puts a teen-aged girl at the center of an interesting dilemma—with nothing less than the survival of the entire human race at stake!

One of the things I have always enjoyed about Henry Melton's books is that they feature intelligent, self-reliant teens who are by and large able to solve their own problems. There is nothing juvenile in how these young-adult novels are put together. Henry Melton is a master storyteller, and I will be anxiously awaiting his next work."

Chris Meadows TeleRead

Follow That Mouse

by Henry Melton

ISBN 978-0-9802253-7-2

Dot Comal loved her home town, although the Utah ranching community of Ranch Exit was too small to call a 'town'. She had her horse, Pokey, and her father to care for, and Ned from the next ranch over was comfortable to be around when he showed up on his motorcycle. But things were changing. The animals, and even her father, were showing signs of a growing irrational rage. Only Watson Winekia, the old Paiute shaman claimed any knowledge of what was happening, but he was too old and he expected Dot to heal the valley. She was at a loss, until a strange mouse led her to bigger secrets than she'd ever imagined, hidden below her feet. She had to wield mysteries hidden for decades quickly, before her home town and everything she loved was wiped off the map!

☙

"The plot was very unique and mind-boggling. Although it is sci-fi, it didn't feel extremely fantastical or out there because it had a realistic set up. Dot's world didn't change overnight, but there were signs and clues which foreshadowed a bigger-than-her conflict."(: ISA :) mixturesbooks.blogspot.com

"Follow that Mouse is sprinkled with interesting, seemingly factual info, while the mysterious impression of odd events turns more serious and gives way to a gripping, constantly evolving (literally!) story that is both intelligent and thought-provoking, disturbing and startling in its revelations. Ned and Dot's relationship is comfortable and real, and the revealed villain has a classic, yet distinctive and creative feel to it - not in a comical sense, to be clear, as this villain is BAD. This is a truly unpredictable, refreshing, and super smart YA sci-fi/ fantasy novel that is entertaining, and at the same time expects you to exercise your brain. Follow that Mouse is surprising right up to the end, and keeps you guessing just as long. I highly recommend it!!!"

Angie L Bibliophilesupportgroup.

Pixie Dust

by Henry Melton

ISBN 978-0-9802253-8-9

Jenny Quinn's life was on course for her advanced physics degree until a lab experiment in vacuum decay turned her life upside down. With career hopes destroyed and her professor dead in an unexplained fall, she is forced to cope with a strange change in her own body. With nothing but her own resources, a childhood infatuation with old comic books may be her only guide to help solve the twin mysteries of cutting edge physics and the murder of her professor, before one or the other puzzle gets her killed.

Henry Melton, award winning author of the YA adventures Emperor Dad and Lighter Than Air, takes us on an adventure with a slightly older heroine, even if she is just four foot ten and everyone calls her Tinkerbell.

www.ingramcontent.com/pod-product-compliance
Lightning Source LLC
Chambersburg PA
CBHW071152260626
47162CB00003B/1014